STRUMMING THE DREAMS OF THE DEAD
AND OTHER STRANGE TALES

BY

CANDLEWRAITH

" Since my youth I felt that stories were floating invisibly all around. The right sensitivity, frame of mind and circumstance enabled me to capture one and make it flow from my pencil to paper. I used to sit in the dark with only candlelight at my desk, hoping for inspiration or such a magical connection. Not much of a stretch from there to believe in ghosts."

Candlewraith

CONTENTS

BUYER BEWARE

Halfway through renovating his home in rural Pennsylvania Jacob Moran found a hidden room. It was tucked between a bedroom and the basement stairs. Judging by size it might originally have been intended as a half bath or walk-in closet, with one strange quirk. The ceiling was extremely low, no more than five feet tall. He had to hunch his shoulders once he entered through the narrow opening he had made with his sledgehammer.

Having no windows and it being a dark, rainy afternoon he relied on the beam of his old Maglite to search the room. It revealed yellowed plaster flecked with an alarming amount of insects and insect parts. They had the look of having been deliberately crushed against the walls. It gave him the creeps.

How the hell could so many insects get in here? Where did they come from? Panning his light slowly he checked the floorboards. There were no obvious gaps or holes in the floor. The ceiling was finished with no cracks or openings. There was no heat or air vent of any kind. There was a square door in the center up above, however, similar to the access panel of an attic. It was closed and seemed a tight fit, and didn't explain how thousands of insects could find entry here. Yet the odd height dimension of the room certainly left space for another mystery up above.

The cement floor was badly stained. In one far corner was a mound of old magazines stacked haphazardly. It was as tall as Jacob's knees. The shadow from it created by his light against the wall looked like an eerie, miniature stalagmite. Some of the issues could easily be collector's items. He could read the same year---1932, on the covers and spines of most. As he reached for them he heard a scratching noise like the sound of a dog or cat begging to be let in. His flashlight and eyes fixed on the panel directly overhead, and a chilling fear pulsed through him.

The sheer oddity of the moment sent him racing toward the narrow opening through which he had come. Being hunched over slowed him, and his arms slapped awkwardly against the walls. As he risked a look back he saw the panel fall to the floor. Dust motes exploded like mushroom clouds. His heart lodged in his throat as a pale face hung upside down through the opening. Black, unblinking eyes focused intently on him, but it made no sound. Then with one white hand it took hold of the molding and jumped spider-like into the room.

Jacob's spine turned to water. The thing faced him, snarling with wickedly sharp teeth. It turned its head slightly and opened its thin mouth so insanely wide it seemed the head would split in two. A stench of corpses and sulfur filled the room. Then it spewed millions of insects with incredible velocity.

With a roaring sound every insect imaginable struck walls and ceiling. Jacob reached the door in the plaster. He launched himself through. Falling and dragging himself down the hall in pure terror he saw the face appear at the opening. He had been naïve to think himself safe once he got free of the room. Yet in the blink of a moment the thing gnashed its teeth and flew at him, biting into his left leg. The pain was electric.

Scrambling to his feet Jacob kicked free and fled toward the kitchen. The thing chasing him seemed to delight in his fear, pursuing him relentlessly. With the speed it had shown it could have been on him immediately. Mind spinning, Jacob grabbed the sharpest knife from the island block; a can of aerosol lacquer and a disposable lighter from his tool cupboard. He made it to the back door and unlocked the deadbolt. If his weapons didn't work he needed an escape route.

Finally, it faced him. Knuckles white from gripping the knife as he stood with his back against the door he got his first full look at the creature. Disbelief flooded through him like the burn of strong liquor, but his fear never wavered. Not for a fleeting second did he doubt the thing meant to kill him. Yet what stood before him should have been inanimate.

For the first time in his life he understood his sister's odd fear of dolls. And this was no store-bought, porcelain or plastic version in a party dress. Every scrap of this thing had been sewn together by hand, except for the black button eyes and scraggly tufts of hair made of God-knows-what. Whoever had made it, or at the very least, walled it up in its tomb back in 1932, had left no warning. Yet he had seen it hurl insects with the speed of unleashed evils from freaking Pandora's Box, and blood ran from a two inch gash in his calf. He wasn't about to give it another chance.

It circled the butcher block island, eyeing a cleaver hanging overhead. Seizing the moment Jacob took the aerosol can from under his arm and fired, setting it aflame with his lighter. The whoosh was deafening. Quick as the little creature scrambled it couldn't outmaneuver fire and was instantly enveloped. The stench of burning straw stung Jacob's eyes and nostrils. He flung open the back door as the thing emitted a freakish scream and writhed on the kitchen floor.

Jacob waited for the fire to go out. The doll had stopped moving long before that, but he wanted to be sure. His tile floor was blackened. Bits of ash fluttered everywhere in the air as he slowly approached the mess. Hunkering down beside it he prodded the thing with his knife. Bits of burned cloth flaked off. Rubbing his beard for a moment to weigh his options Jacob decided it was in his best interest to push the issue. He had to try and finish it off somehow, or at the very least, secure it or limit its mobility. He pressed the blade into the doll's abdomen, pinning it to the floor. The mouth flew open and deadly teeth snapped as it flailed about.

Cursing, he glanced around the kitchen. There was nothing in the immediate area that would do. Testing the firmness of the knife in the floor he decided to risk leaving briefly. He jogged to his bedroom closet and returned with the small steel safe Sarah had given him for his baseball card collection. The doll was still squirming, half-melted black eyes staring up at him with malice. Jacob slid the tumblers to open the lock. His precious cards in their protective sheets seemed like his last lifeline to a sane world. He set them carefully on the far counter. Clenching his jaw he set the case next to the thing and rubbed his hands together to focus. This next move would be tricky.

With one swift motion he freed the knife tip from the floor and swept the skewered doll perfectly into the chamber. He slammed the lid, ripping his knife free, and spun the tumblers, locking the damned thing safely inside. He could hear its nails scratching against the interior, but he let go a big breath of air and let himself finally relax as he leaned against the seared cupboard. After a moment he reached over to the fridge, grabbed a beer and downed it quickly.

"Who the hell would ever believe this?" he asked the room.

The safe went still, as if the thing inside was trying to lure him into opening it. When that tactic failed it screamed again, nails digging at the steel. Jacob's mind raced. He couldn't be sure how long the safe would hold.

The situation was insane. He had read about inanimate objects being possessed but never given it a second thought. All he knew was that he had to get this thing out of his house. He was afraid even that wouldn't be enough. For all he knew he could drive thirty miles out of town to fling the case off a bridge to rocky waters below, only to come home and find the demonic doll waiting for him. TV shows and bad horror films had poisoned his hope.

He had to provide another target---another human for it to focus its evil upon. This wasn't something he took lightly, but he trusted no other option. He cleaned his wound. It had an odd, musty smell that worried him. He grabbed the safe and another beer and headed for the living room. Once the computer booted up he signed onto eBay. He had bought a few things online now and then-- new electronic equipment; tools and occasional collectible items for Sarah before she had left him. He had browsed the categories enough to know that there was a huge market for the paranormal. Plenty of sellers banked on that angle and threw together intricate stories of their haunted jewelry and knick knacks to get in on the action, but it had never occurred to him that any of it might be true. With any luck there were buyers out there who recognized the genuine article and knew how to handle it. Otherwise he would be unleashing this madness on innocent victims.

Jacob logged in and began writing his story. There was no need to embellish. The only error he had made was in not snapping a photo of the thing pinned to his floor. Getting a shot now was out of the question. He photographed the safe with his ashen handprints all over it and snapped a close-up of the knife. The blade was black with soot. He thought about getting a pic of his bite wound also, but decided against it. Too much might scare potential buyers away or make folks think he was running an ad campaign for an new horror film.

After uploading the photos he submitted his one-day listing for one hundred dollars. It was an official auction now. He was fairly sure the box and shipping material he had kept from his last purchase were a perfect fit for the portable safe. All he had to do was wait. The safe lay quiet beside him as he ate lunch while reading sports updates online. Twice he went back into the kitchen to stare at the burn-scarred floor to remind himself that the incident had really happened and that he hadn't completely lost his mind.

He nearly jumped out of his skin when his phone received a text message. He had included his number in the listing in case potential buyers had questions, which was a calculated risk. Any nutball could contact him, but if there was any chance to speed up the process of getting the doll out of his life he was willing to take a little shit.

"Bring it on." he whispered.

Twenty-three crank messages came that first hour. Jacob almost stopped reading them, but a couple were so amusing amidst all the idiots that it helped pass the time. And then the next one hit home. It was from a Darrell Auerbach, associate professor at a small university in Rhode Island. He taught clinical psychiatry as well as courses on shaman studies and demonic possession, and was interested in Jacob's discovery. He made a request: provide further proof of the doll through photos or video of the secret room in exchange for a serious bid.

Swallowing hard, Jacob set his camera to video record and slid in his 8 GB memory card. He found a large box complete with shipping material and packed the safe tightly inside, leaving no margin for movement. He then pressed the record button and held up the camera to capture himself.

"This better be a legit offer, Auerbach," he said with deadly seriousness, "because I really don't want to go back in there."

He let the camera be his eyes through the sledgehammer-made entrance. The walls were still black with thousands of insects stuck to them. Hundreds more lined the floor where they had fallen. A chilling numbness struck him and his eyes began to tear as he saw that the panel was no longer on the floor where he had last seen it, but had somehow been returned to its place in the ceiling. It was pulled shut just as when he had first discovered the room.

"Not doing it, Auerbach," the camera view panned back and forth as Jacob shook his head. "Not going up there. Not for all the money in the world."

His mind raced, envisioning himself fetching a chair and taking that panel down. Anything could happen, from finding a hidden treasure to having another damn doll start feasting on his face while he was vulnerable. No way in hell he was going up there.

"You're welcome to bring a team and check this out yourself," he told the camera, but all he really wanted was for this whole thing to be over. Once he got the safe on its way he would sell the house cheap to the first buyer and get as far away as possible

He got a close-up of the date on the magazines and then turned off the camera. The scratching sound echoed through the panel suddenly, and he almost crapped his pants hurrying to the exit. Just as he reached it a small face appeared there from out in the hallway, looking in. Several others appeared behind it, slit-like mouths starting to open.

The secret attic had housed more than one. Once he had broken into the room they had probably scattered through this end of the house and been lying in wait in his bedroom, bath and closets.

They pinned him to the floor and forced his mouth open. One straddled him and slowly opened its own foul mouth. Jacob knew he would never get out alive. With a savage lunge it placed its mouth over Jacob's and expelled the blast of a million insects.

****

Lisa Moran stood in her father's living room surveying the work she had ahead of her. A neighbor had reported him missing and the police had become involved, but there was no trace of her father. She and he had not been close, but the disappearance puzzled her. She knew he had been working on upgrading the house. There were signs of that: the living room had been recently painted and the patio landscaped, but the kitchen was a mess. It looked as though there might have been a small, contained fire. The officer who had escorted her inside had even commented on it. No foul play was indicated, so her father's status remained simply missing.

As she was going through his things she heard a phone alert. It was like the sound her own phone when she received text messages. Searching, she tracked it to a box of books on the living room floor. She found it, still receiving a message. It was from a Gail Peterson in Ohio who ran an antique shop.

Curious, Lisa wrote back, and the women exchanged pleasantries about their children. In the course of their chat the stranger explained that she had been the last-minute, high-bidder on an item Jacob had for auction on eBay. She had already sent the payment through Paypal and forwarded Lisa the transaction details.

The story seemed legitimate. Lisa had noticed a large box ready for shipping on the coffee table. She talked for a few minutes more and promised to drop off the package at the post office when she went into town for dinner.

As she was headed out the door her father's phone received another message. It was an odd request. Some professor in Rhode Island was interested in the house. A buyer would certainly make Lisa's life easier. She even remembered seeing her father's digital camera in the back bedroom near the stairs. As soon as she got back from dinner she would tour all the rooms and get up close and personal shots of its nooks and crannies.

MADD WORLD

'Most of us don't dwell on what can happen behind closed doors. It's easier to shut out what we would rather not face. News coverage brings grim reminders, but we still breathe easy until something happens in our own town, or down the block, or in the old apartment complex across the street. Then we can't escape the realization of how cruel we can be to each other. Then it dawns on us that evil exists.'

Melanie Norwood stopped typing and read what she had written. She considered herself lucky. She worked from home, doing online medical billing. That in itself cut out the expense of a work wardrobe and commuting. She chose her hours and cranked out the numbers. The rest of her time was her own. Writing articles and blogs on the side gave her extra cash.

She lived alone. A deep-seated self-defense mechanism kept her from getting close to anyone. She was polite in her journeys to the market for groceries. She exchanged pleasantries with neighbors when she saw them, and knew food delivery people by name. To the casual observer she was a happy soul. Considering her childhood she was quite well-adjusted, but her existence was solitary without a partner or children. Basically, she lived online.

Taking a break from writing she fixed herself an iced tea and got comfortable at the computer. She visited her usual haunts--- Twitter and Facebook, working her farm in Farm Town and chatting with Gloria and Dave. Things were pretty much as usual until she got a notification someone had written on her profile page.

"Who in the hell is Kelly Maddison?" she asked herself. Clicking over she felt her face go slack as the page loaded and the words jumped off the screen at her.

Stupid photos, with stupid comments. Did you copy some kid's page on MySpace?

Writing down the username she removed the post, wondering if any of her friends had seen it. No one had mentioned anything. Taking a deep breath to calm herself she typed the name in the search function and was quickly directed to the attacker's page.

Kelly Maddison, listed as female, 24 years old. No location, and her profile photo was a black and white drawing of the Mad Hatter from Alice in Wonderland.

"Figures," she said softly with a nod.

Mel had never been targeted by a flamer before. Careful not to respond she went back to her own business. She lost an hour surfing eBay in various categories. When she checked her mail there was a glaring notification that K. Maddison had left another comment on her Facebook Wall.

"Shit," she spat, kicking herself for not using the block feature. She expected more sniping drivel, but what she read almost knocked her off her chair.

I know where you live. I can get into your house. At night. While you sleep.

In disbelief she stared at the lines for several minutes. Then she went into action, taking a screenshot of the threat and saving it in her mail, complete with all the pertinent info. She removed the post from her personal page, then went to her privacy settings.

After scanning the instructions for blocking people she added Ms Maddison to her block list and breathed a sigh of relief. But she didn't stop there. She searched for an address to contact the Facebook administrators and reported the abuse.

The incident left her feeling dirty. She left the computer for a while to do her laundry and tidy up a bit, and caught herself glancing out the windows to look around. It struck her odd the person had mentioned a house, specifically. It was a slightly general term, but these days a lot of people lived in apartments. Was it just a lucky guess?

As doubt haunted her Mel jumped back online and Googled her own name. Not only did it come up, but so did her address. With a couple quick clicks of the mouse anyone could zoom in on Google Earth and see her street and the front of her house up close and personal.

"Jesus," she whispered, as waves of panic fluttered inside her chest.

Response from Facebook a couple of hours later was a surprisingly unconcerned form letter. Block the violator, yada yada. That should resolve the problem. If not, here's a link where you can fill out a more in-depth complaint.

Ok, she had done that. She felt a little better, but still made rounds checking to make sure all the doors and windows were locked. She knew this Maddison person probably lived on the other side of the country and simply took pleasure in shocking others from the safe anonymity of their own computer. It happened all the time. Yet she almost wished she had followed her sister's advice when she first moved in and gotten a dog.

'Screw that,' she told herself. Damned if she was going to let a freak mess with her life. She puttered in the kitchen, making herself a nice dinner and watching an old Golden Girls episode on her portable TV. When everything was ready she carried it into her bedroom to eat at the computer. She had forums to check and needed a nice, mindless game or two.

She couldn't resist checking, and all was quiet on Facebook. She had nearly finished planting a crop of onions in her Farm Town account when the little red notice popped up to alert her of new activity. As she clicked on it for the particulars the thought flashed through her head that the menace could easily have created a new account.

But it wasn't a new user, and it wasn't one of her friends. Kelly Maddison had posted another message to her.

"What?" Mel's incredulous voice boomed in the quiet house.

Collecting herself, she clicked on Maddison's name first, and was re-directed to the woman's page. The profile photo had been changed. John Tenniel's classic illustration of the Mad Hatter was gone. In its place was a horrific, color drawing of the Hatter holding a bloody knife as he approached a young Alice tied to a bed.

Her eyes stung with shock. Quickly she checked her block list, but there were no names there. Either there had been a glitch and the name had been kicked out, or this odd person had found a way to beat the system. Mel typed in the name again and blocked her. She went back to check several times to make sure it was still there.

Off with her head.... the idiot had written. Even deleted it still rang in Mel's ears.

She popped in on a forum or two briefly and then hit Pogo to play a few games. During the fourth frame of bowling she noticed her name mentioned in the small chat box. Her *real* name, not the username members saw on Pogo.

You can't get rid of me that easily, Mel.

The user was Hatter666. Closing her browser Melanie stared at her desktop for several moments. Fidgeting in her chair she wasn't sure what to do, and finally decided to take her dishes into the kitchen. She checked all the doors and windows again. The house was quiet. To give herself a little more peace of mind she decided to fetch her old hockey stick from the hall closet. God knows she couldn't trust putting a kitchen knife under her pillow. The way she tossed and turned she'd be shredded by morning.

As she made her way back through the kitchen to shut off the light something caught her eye. She froze in her tracks, mouth open, as the blood drained from her face. A drink container from a fast food joint stood on the counter. Beads of moisture rolled silently down its side.

With a panicky swivel she scanned the kitchen but found nothing else out of place. She tightened her grip on the hockey stick and cocked it shoulder high. The drink was still there, but it seemed odd somehow, almost flickering like a hologram poised on the counter. Her fear must be short-circuiting her reality.

She tried to call out her brother's name but sound wouldn't come. Swallowing, she tried again. There was a million to one chance he might have swung by and used his emergency key. He had done it once before several years ago. Mel clung to that hope.

"James?" her strained voice was full of fear.

No answer came. Eerie stillness pulsed around her. With agonizing slowness she forced herself to move through the house, re-checking doors and windows and possible hiding places. The air felt heavy and seemed to be mocking her.

She had checked everywhere except her bedroom. Hesitating at the doorway she glanced in, eyes darting to find an intruder. There was a playing card---the Queen of Hearts, face up on the seat of her computer chair, and then several other cards on the floor in a trail toward her bed. Mel inched closer, scanning the bedspread. Nothing there. She looked down at the cards again. The last one she could see was several inches *under* the bed frame. There was movement in the shadows under there, and it was as if someone pulled the ripcord on one of her deepest childhood fears.

In her frantic haste to get the hell out she slammed backwards against her closet door. The hockey stick knocked the wind out of her. She dropped to the rug, trying desperately to get air that never seemed to come. When the spasm finally eased she managed to focus again.

Kelly Maddison crawled out from under the bed with the insane agility of a spider, eyes dark and swimming with hate. There was something wrong with her neck. Her teeth were clamped down on a knife handle as she scuttled out and loomed over Mel.

Her face was incredibly pale and lacked definitive features. It wavered like mist, and Mel realized there was no color, only shades of gray. There was also nothing solid below the broken neck but a rippling black mass.

The bedroom door closed.

MIDNIGHT AT THE PSYCHOMANTIUM

Jake Lowry found a flyer in his mailbox a week before Halloween. It's lurid, yellow paper with black, art deco skulls and ravens peaked his interest, and the further he read the more intrigued he became. He was pretty familiar with the gas lamp district downtown. He often hit the rare bookstores and record shops along 3rd Avenue. One of his card club memberships there had probably forwarded the flyer based on his genre tastes. Still, in all his excursions he had never seen any theater called the PSYCHOMANTIUM.

Grabbing a beer from the fridge he parked himself on the sofa with flyer in hand. On Halloween they were showing classic horror films. Twenty-five bucks cover charge would get him in to see *Eraserhead*; *Suspiria*; the original *Texas Chainsaw Massacre*; *Curse of the Demon*; and *Freaks*. Best of all, they were slated to run Van Langdon's *Whispers of Evil*, an extremely rare film based on the unsolved Villisca axe murders in 1912. Jake had been trying to see that for years. There was actually a huge debate still raging between factions of the horror industry on whether or not the movie had indeed been made or was pure legend.

The first film was set to show at 9 PM, with no admittance once it started. Free hot dog buffet and soda. Anyone in costume was eligible for the grand prize drawing, which featured an undisclosed, authenticated prop from one of the films. His mind raced with the possibilities. Even if it wasn't something he wanted for his own collection he could no doubt sell it at online auction.

Fishing his cell phone from his pocket he hit speed dial. Rita was just down the hall in 314, but a stickler for her privacy. Her policy was to answer the door with a baseball bat if anyone paid an unannounced visit. Her left-handed swing was legendary.

"Speak," her pleasant voice answered quickly.

"They're coming to get you, Bar…bara," he deadpanned into the mouthpiece. It was one of his favorite lines from *Night of the Living Dead.*

"Hey," she replied without the usual horror film response. "I'm on my way out the door. What's up?"

"Ah, ok. I just wanted to see if you got that flyer in the mail today. I can catch you later."

"Only have a minute. You talking Ming's Chinese or Chip the Whip's Porn Shop?"

"Hilarious," he smirked. He could imagine her tapping impatient fingers along the galloping rat tattoo on the back of her neck.

"Yellow flyer for a place called the PSYCHOMANTIUM," he said quickly. "Downtown somewhere. What are you doing on Halloween? I meant to ask sooner but with our work schedules lately I keep missing you."

She was interested but had a family party she couldn't blow off. The theater was a mystery to her as well, but she did suggest taking the bus rather than risk parking his car in the gas lamp overnight. It made sense. By the time the movies ended the buses would be running again. Rita had offered to come after her commitment, which he would have loved, but the no admittance once the film started policy made that impossible. She suggested calling Deuce and Tim, but Deuce's band was playing The Bitter End that night. Tim was going to some frat party. Normally Jake had no problem going alone, but was hoping to share the experience with a horror fan. As he hung up he promised to fill her in on the details.

The week sped by. Weather turned cold by California standards as the days played out under a chilly, leaden sky. It was perfect for Halloween, which fell on Saturday for the first time in ages. As the afternoon wound its way toward twilight Jake turned the TV to the Ghost Hunters marathon and sat by the window. His upstairs apartment looked out over the entrance to the complex. From his view he could watch the little kids in Target costumes pulling their parents along the sidewalk in their excited quest for candy.

His make-up had come out perfect. The Ghoul kit he had picked up in the mall Halloween store had been easier than he expected, making his lip appear split apart and his eyes demented. The skin tone was a slightly greenish white of which he was quite proud. A gaping wound in his neck and dark, ratty clothes from the thrift store completed the image, along with a little cottage cheese and ketchup to give the effect of brain matter on his shoes.

Rita had called earlier to check in. She was the only one who knew Halloween had been his sister's birthday. Only she knew his childhood memories of trick or treating with Kate; that his sis had died in a freak accident when a railing gave way at a famous attraction on Halloween, and that every year Jake drank a toast to her at the exact time of her birth. He set the alarm on his watch, locked the front door and stepped outside as shadows started to thicken over the neighborhood.

His spirits were high as he drank in the sights and sounds of Wyndham Street. East of his apartment building was an older section of stone porches aglow with flickering, carved pumpkins. Wind chime witches sang on the light breeze and carried the aroma of apple cider with cinnamon sticks. A kid could score awesome candy from those houses.

The homes were more modern to the west of his apartment. Eaves fluttered with fake cobwebs and sensor-activated spiders with blinking, red eyes. A fog machine pulsed eerie vapors across the way at the Williams house, and in shadow behind the front gate an animatronic zombie grabbed at passers-by. A couple of cars pulled up and costumed kids spilled out. A nice party was about to get underway.

Memories stirred from hibernation and held up images like flashcards. He visualized himself and Kate back in their old neighborhood, eyes wide with wonder at the magic of Halloween. There was something about that one night of the year and all its trappings that called to Jake, even if he couldn't understand why. He felt more alive, more tuned in to everything. Every decoration and nuance of the holiday caught his eye. Maybe it had something to do with being turned loose on the streets at night. Back then things were safer, or at least *felt* safer. Halloween just seemed to make so many more things possible.

The bus was on time. As he paid his fare the driver held out a bucket of candy. Jake took a mini Snickers and chose a seat near the back. It had started off as a good ride. Several of the younger passengers were dressed in costumes headed for parties. Most got off at the Broadway stop. Once the bus turned off the main avenue of shops and restaurants the scenery changed dramatically. Graffiti and dead weeds were prevalent under the streetlights as the dark of a crisp evening settled in. At Seventh and C Street an older man with long, unkempt hair got on. He gestured rudely and blew angry darts through an invisible straw at passing cars, then repeated the routine at fellow passengers. As long as the fellow remained up front Jake figured no harm, no foul.

He had charted the route online and knew his stop was next. As he pulled the chord to alert the driver his eyes raced worriedly over a ghastly, spray-painted rendition of Charles Manson's face looming from a block wall. Red lettering that had been heavily spayed to allow dripping like real blood spelled out vulgar, paranoid phrases. Jake had never studied the Tate-LaBianca murders from the late '60's, but knew enough to clench his jaw and question the motive of such a design.

"I hope you have a knife on you, son," the driver said grimly as Jake stepped down and the door closed behind him. The bus sped off faster than usual.

It was too late to turn back. Thirty minutes before another bus would come. He didn't relish waiting around. There were homeless people around every corner, or faces in shadow making deals and flitting away like roaches at the sound of his footsteps. He swallowed hard and hurried on, eyes speedballing on everything to stay alert and protect himself and still search out his destination.

Halfway up the block he could see spires of what looked like an old gothic church through a cluster of trees. "Sanctuary!" rang through his brain. Someone inside might be able to direct him to the theater. That, or pray for his soul, he grimaced.

He should have done a dry run of this trip during daylight. His own reflection in a dirty, warehouse window nearly gave him a heart attack. He had completely forgotten he was in costume. The fake brain matter on his black shoes had dried and looked more like old bird shit. Taking a deep breath, he brushed low-hanging fringe of trees aside and began climbing a cracked stone stair. Bleak holes in the pavement hinted of where a railing had been removed, most likely against the assault of skateboards.

Darkness was deepening. The old-fashioned, gas lampposts threw weak, atmospheric light that pulsed like sputtering torches. Jake was stunned as he glanced up at the church façade. In actuality it was a run-of-the-mill, rectangular building, but some artist with mad skills had painted it to look like a genuine, gothic church, complete with flying buttresses, stained glass windows and two eerie stone ravens perched overhead on a mammoth arch. Even the background had been painted in the greatest detail with the effects of moonlight and shadows to give the appearance of a midnight scene. His mind flashed to intricate sidewalk art he had seen recently on the net. The realism of depth perception made those works completely believable. This illusion had been fashioned in that same vein, and exquisitely executed.

Something rustled tall, dead weeds against the warehouse next door. Jake's hand flew to the painted knob. His shoulder hit the door panel as he pushed his way in and pulled the door closed behind him. As he turned to face the entrance it was as if he had been transported in time. He stood in a massive, grand theater lobby from the 1930's or '40's, or one that had been grand once but had fallen into shabbiness. It was dimly lit by comedy and tragedy mask-shaped wall sconces. Silhouettes of dead flies and spiders were visible inside each frosted glass. The worn carpet was deep purple. Original promotional posters of the classic horror films he had come to see had been crudely taped to the gray walls between dusty, marble columns. Those stretched up into a high ceiling veiled in shadow.

"Welcome to the PSYCHOMANTIUM, sir," a thin voice whispered so close to Jake's ear that he shuddered involuntarily and took a quick step back.

A gaunt man with long, silver hair hanging straight down past bony shoulders was staring at him eagerly. There were deep hollows beneath his gray eyes that did not look like make-up. He wore a dark suit with a jeweled spider on his lapel. His thinness reminded Jake of addiction or severe illness, but it was the long, gnarly hands that were the most frightening of all. Filthy and caked with what appeared to be mold and perhaps fresh earth, like a grave-robber's hands, they took Jake's money with the hungry greed of baby vultures. Then the inside of Jake's wrist was quickly stamped with a grinning, red skull logo.

"Uh…not many…not many people here," Jake stammered, still stunned by the suddenness with which the fellow had seemed to appear out of nowhere.

"Early yet, sir," the man licked his thin lips. He raised a crooked finger to point left toward a dark archway past the *Eraserhead* poster. "You have time to browse the exhibit. There you can visit our food and drink tables and find the auditorium where the films will be shown."

Jake started toward the arch. After a step or two he swung back around, thinking to ask the man if he knew what the grand prize in the giveaway might be. He hadn't even been given a ticket, he realized. But the man had disappeared. It didn't seem possible he could have walked that huge floor to be out of sight in such a short time. Staring in each direction Jake found no trace of him. There was only a small, white moth apparently injured or dying where the man had stood, rapidly fluttering its wings that caused it to spin in a circle over the dark carpet.

"Exhibit?" Jake whispered to himself. There had been a line at the bottom of the flyer, he remembered. Something about entertainment in the spirit of Halloween that he had taken to mean a party atmosphere. Unless there was some hidden trap door nearby he still couldn't explain the man's sudden disappearance. But he was safely indoors with the promise of food and films just ahead. There was probably still time to inquire about the giveaway. He suspected this was going to be a Halloween to remember.

The distinct aroma of warm hotdogs wafted down the corridor and led him on. As he entered the sparse new room Jake stepped onto antique, parquet flooring. The design was quite stunning: winged gargoyles in a pattern of four at each corner of an ornate box. Six long, aluminum folding tables had been set up against the wall directly to his right and were spilling over with food. He took a thick, Styrofoam plate and sampled it all. The spread was amazing, with every condiment and side dish imaginable. Only as he stepped aside to begin eating did he notice the odd fact that no one had been jostling him at the covered, metal hot dog warmer. No one had impeded him at all.

It was more than a little odd, but the food was great. As he scarfed deviled eggs and freshened his soda he caught sight of a directional arrow taped to the bare wall. 'Auditorium," someone had written inside the arrow in spidery handwriting. Beneath it was a neatly typed list of the films and their running times. 'Grand prize tickets handed out at 9 sharp!' had been scrawled in large letters at the bottom.

His watch said eight-fifteen. Forty-five minutes to kill. Restocking his plate he followed the sign, turning down a short hall that opened into a narrow holding area that was similar in décor to the main lobby.

The lighting was yellowish and dim, adding to the effect of stomach-turning wonder as Jake's eyes flew from one display table to the next. Freakish tissue floated in dirty jars of formaldehyde. Glass cases held severed limbs. Coffins so old one could almost hear their sighs of desiccation presented small figures not possibly of this earth.

"Rita will kill me if I don't get pics." he whispered to himself.

Setting his drink down he gripped his plate carefully and flipped open his cell phone. A quick glance around revealed no employees anywhere in the vicinity, but two others in costume at opposite ends of the exhibit. He had not noticed them before. Both were male. The one leaning in close to inspect a mummified cat with two heads was dressed as Pinhead from the *Hellraiser* films. It was an awesome mask and make-up job. Thousands of pins sprouted from the skull and looked incredibly real. The fellow couldn't be much older than eighteen.

The other, perhaps in his late thirties, Jake estimated, was a vampire. His costume recreated the classic Lugosi version, complete with black cape snaking along the floor as he walked softly beside the shark-woman display. Thousands of pointed, Great White teeth jutting out from her oval mouth gleamed even in the low light of the exhibit room and made Jake shudder. He had to get a shot of it, and tiptoed forward as the man moved on.

As he zoomed in on the woman's face a parasitic worm crawled from her open mouth. Jake spasmed in reaction, snapping the picture out of pure reflex. The thing had a fluted head and was as big around as a USB cable. It reared up several times, showing him its wicked mouth and sucking disks used to attach to its host, then whipped around behind the shark-woman's head and was lost from sight.

Jake's heart was still slamming against his chest as he glanced around the room. No one else had seen. He checked the picture he had taken. He had captured a perfect image of the thing poised like a cobra between her jagged teeth.

"Holy freaking shit," he whispered to himself, and took a deep breath. He could imagine Rita lampooning him for being so scared, and made himself take a few more photos. He did so holding the camera phone at arm's length and keeping an eye on his surroundings. By the time he was finished the others had already moved on. He might regret it later, but for now he dumped his plate in a trashcan against the wall and followed the arrow to the auditorium.

The hallway was shrouded in darkness. An usher in a red jacket stood at its far end beneath a weak, overhead lamp. His face was hidden behind a turned up collar with a dark cap tugged forward, but his eyes glowed like hot embers in a bed of ash. He checked Jake's wrist for the skull stamp and waved him on silently.

As Jake passed by he noticed the fellow's nametag read 'Caligari'.

"Nice," Jake whispered with a nod as he came to black, double doors. An art deco silver skull had been hand-painted in their center so that the icon split perfectly in half when pulled open. His chest fluttered a little with anticipation as he gripped one of the metal handles. The hardware was loose and clattered as he pulled for access, giving him his first glimpse of the auditorium.

He stepped into the narrow entry, following dark purple carpet around a turn that opened up his entire view. Only half of the house lights were on. The place was enormous. His head swiveled to take it all in---row after rising row of purple seats; three levels of balconies with purple drapery and more pale wall sconces.

Old black and white photos of celebrities long dead were framed on the purple wallpaper--- Max Schreck; Karloff & both Chaney's; Elsa Lanchester and Bette Davis and Peter Cushing. The stage was massive. A brocaded, violet curtain large enough to cover a big ship hid the screen. Silver ravens etched in fine detail perched atop ornamental niches set into the wall at each corner. The disturbing, decrepit lavishness of it all was like something from The Fall of the House of Usher.

"As if Vincent Price and Prince came together to design a movie theater..." he muttered, snapping more photos for Rita.

To his great surprise the theater was nearly empty. Six, maybe seven other people were strewn around the auditorium. Two couples, one way down front. They were dressed Goth with all the trimmings. Cloaks and plates of food and studded, leather boots took up seats beside and in front of them. Jake didn't envy their spines that view.

The other twosome was male. One was talking on a cell phone while the other was polishing off a monstrous pile of nachos. They were costumed as Jigsaw and Leatherface.

The young man dressed as Pinhead was up in the nearest balcony. The Lugosi vampire was far left at the end of an aisle halfway up. Someone else seemed to be seated in the back, but blended in against the shadowy draperies than ran floor to ceiling. Any limber soul could have climbed down from the top balcony via that route, depending on the strength of its fixtures. Jake couldn't help wondering what sort of spider nest might be tucked away in there. He also couldn't fathom why more people hadn't shown, or how this place could afford to host such an event with so little to show for it. He sighed, hoping they weren't about to return the admission fee. He was dying to see these films.

Staking out an area close to the middle of the auditorium he veered right so as not to infringe on the vampire dude. He chose the best of three aisle seats and eased himself down, getting comfortable. It was going to be a long night. If memory served the flyer had mentioned that trips to the food bar between films were allowed. He would be ready again after the first one. He already regretted not bringing his drink.

He was factoring his odds of making it there and back when a figure loped onto the stage. Whoever it was earned points for realism. A better wolf-creature Jake had never seen. He could feel the heat of its stare drilling into him even three hundred feet away. It's tongue ran feverishly across its jagged teeth and threads of saliva swung from its jaws. It was extremely unnerving. The Goth chick near the front was hiding her face under her cloak.

The gaunt, dark-suited man with silver hair he had lost in the lobby reappeared through a trap door center stage. As a bluish-white spotlight spilled over him he held up a huge roll of orange tickets. The wolf did frantic, feral steps around the man. Its eyes were insane, but as a metallic chiming sounded throughout the auditorium from an unseen clock at the stroke of nine the creature bolted. It disappeared into the shadows behind the stage. Jake was not sorry to see it go. He had not dared take its picture for Rita.

"I will come to your seats and hand you your tickets," the gaunt man strained the veins in his throat to be heard.

"What's the prize?" Pinhead screamed from the balcony. The voice reminded Jake of pot and pimple cream.

"One of you," the gravedigger replied using his best game-show announcer voice, "will win something quite unique. A prize not obtainable elsewhere. To our winner goes the very axe used by the unknown monster responsible for the deaths of eight people in June of 1912. It was used as a prop in Whispers of Evil, but make no mistake. This is the real thing."

"An actual murder weapon?" the Goth girl asked incredulously, and with obvious disdain.

"What have you been smokin', Pops? There's no way," Pinhead's voice screeched through the Auditorium. "That axe has changed hands more than a fucking Darryl Strawberry trading card. It's literally been swapped for a friggin' box of chocolates. If that's not proof the world is insane I don't know what is. But it's locked up at the Historical Society in Iowa. If you have an axe, it's a fake."

The gravedigger smiled. "A little knowledge is a dangerous thing," his eyes locked onto the boy. "One can recite tales told by others, and accept them as gospel. Or one may have *inside information*. You do not have to accept our prize, should you win."

Jake chuckled to himself. The house lights dimmed severely and threw the auditorium into a darkness quite like a nightly living room with light coming in only from an adjacent kitchen. It took Jake's eyes a minute to adjust. As he squinted at the stage cold, leathery fingers closed over his left ankle.

Erupting out of his chair the seat flew up against its back with a bouncing clatter that reverberated through the huge room. Panicky, Jake searched the dark aisle floor around him but found nothing. He hunkered down, fishing out his keys and switching on the small but high-powered camping flashlight. Empty popcorn boxes and candy wrappers were revealed under its beam, along with other things he wished he had never seen: used condoms and even a dirty syringe. Serpent-like yellow eyes blinked back at him and then disappeared as something crawled back into the farther recesses of seat aisles.

"Happy Halloween," the gravedigger whispered beside him.

Jake's body jerked forward in fright, jamming his knee into the seat frame.

"Don't let our little diversions unnerve you, young man," he said soothingly, squeezing Jake's arm with his filthy, jagged fingers. "It's all in the spirit of Halloween. Here's your prize ticket. Good luck. Now have a seat and enjoy the films. They are quite worth the trip, don't you think?"

Bony hands pressed Jake down into his seat and held out an orange ticket with such exaggerated flair that one would think it guaranteed riches. Jake accepted it and the gravedigger scuttled away down the shadowy aisle. A slight odor of mold lingered behind.

Waving his hand in front of him to move the smelly air Jake contemplated leaving. This place was twisted, and there was no telling what other surprises might come up during the next few hours. Great as they were, he had already seen most of the movies. It was that promise of the Villisca film that kept him in his seat. And limitless trips to the food bar was gravy. With his little flashlight he checked the ticket. The skull logo took up most of the paper, with five numbers inside it. Shrugging, he tucked it carefully away in the breast pocket of his thrift store jacket.

More of the house lights had been dimmed. Only a few still burned around the auditorium like random stars in a night sky. A glance toward the stage revealed that the colossal curtain over the screen had vanished. In its place was the most incredible thing Jake had ever seen.

"What the Hell?" the Pinhead boy voiced Jake's amazement aloud.

Jake seemed to be looking into a universe. A gargantuan mirror hung where the theater screen should have been. Black, tapered candles were attached to the mirror's edge about every six feet, flickering hypnotically due to the motion of air from a large, silent ceiling fan overhead. The light from their flames was just enough to allow Jake to perceive the enigmatic depth of the mirror. He was immediately transfixed. He felt his body going numb as he gazed ' into its center, every molecule of his soul helplessly focused upon it.

He felt lightheaded. As he ventured deeper he seemed to come out the other side of the initial star system, set down in a shadowy hallway that extended indefinitely. Doorways opened up on either side as he walked on. His fellow movie goers from the auditorium were inside, each in their own room, and each embroiled in their own unique struggle. Some battled inner demons from their subconscious; some seemed merely to be lost in bizarre hallucination, and some Jake could only guess were under attack from entities of other realms.

His emotions spilled over in a mix of horror and panic. The Dracula man's eyes begged silently for help as nightmarish creatures cut out his heart, stitched him up and left him to finish his life devoid of love. An invisible barrier of some sort kept Jake from stepping past the threshold. One of the surgeon-things closed the door in his face.

The Goth couple were in adjacent rooms. Jake caught only a brief glimpse of the boy as he vanished beneath the murky, green surface of a lake. The girl's fate was far more intricate. Two figures with expressionless faces hovered over her as she lay on a bed. One used a tiny syringe to shoot something into her veins; the other soaked her head with gallons of bourbon. In between rounds they feigned smothering her with kisses.

As Jake pushed on he came upon the others. He hadn't paid much attention to them in the auditorium, remembering them only as Nachos and Cell Phone. Mr. N. plummeted from the balcony of a high-rise head first. C.P.'s fate, being a *Saw* fan, was creatively twisted, with shifting torments from a plethora of horror films. Jake lingered in that doorway against his own conscious will, almost breathless in abject terror as an Ed Gein clone started measuring the mans face. Bloody curtains were hurriedly closed over the entry to block his view.

The darkness was deeper now, and undulating like rolling waves of night. He was incredibly cold. As he approached another door his ears caught the faint but unnerving sound of something wet dragging itself across a floor. Jake leaned in slightly to investigate, knowing this would be Pinhead's room. Before his eyes had much chance to focus some unnamable thing loomed in the open doorway. It towered over him, had pale gray skin that was moist and spongy and reminded Jake of giant squids. Hundreds of tentacles with suckers opened and closed to reveal razor-sharp teeth.

Putrid slime splattered over him as the thing shook its head and began to ooze toward him. Jake ran, brain screaming with the fleeting image of what he had seen behind the creature. A half circle of gray entities committed vile, perverted acts upon the boy while the once imposing Pinhead mask lay discarded and slack on the stained floor.

Jake ran, heart on fire in his chest despite the numbness in his limbs. The thing was chasing him toward the final door. His door.

With each jarring step the possibilities taunted him—a swarm of spiders on his face; being set on fire; something creeping out from under his bed as he slept and lay vulnerable. He approached the pulsing doorway and tried to run past it but hit an invisible wall. A strong, unseen hand gripped his jaw and turned his head, forcing him to look. His deepest fear was not what he expected.

The enforcers of this sadistic game might just as well have slit all of Jake's major arteries and let blood flow out until he ran dry. It wasn't himself he was made to witness. He saw his sister, who had meant more to him than anything in the world. A large part of himself had died with her. Over the years it had become harder to remember the details of her face, which tormented Jake. He felt something must be wrong with him to fail in keeping her close.

Now, in this cold, undulating darkness that gripped him like a famished demon, he was shown that Kate was damned, suffering eternal tortures. Her eyes were pools of pain, but she shook her head to tell him not to give in. Jake tried to fight. He could sense something creeping up behind him but his legs were stone. As resignation and despair began to wash over him an alarm went off.

He jerked awake, striking his head on the back of his chair. The alarm on his watch was going off, as loud as chimes from a grandfather clock in the utter quiet of the auditorium. Jake bolted from his seat, blood racing like quicksilver in his veins. A frantic glance around him revealed his fellow theater-goers in comatose slumps in their chairs, some drooling, seconds away from compete consumption.

All he could think to do was wrench the metal flashlight from his keys, running headlong toward the stage. Without gazing into the mirror he hurled his weapon with every ounce of strength left in him.

His aim was true. The clink of one small section breaking set off a domino effect. Large chunks crashed down in a deafening avalanche of glass. It flew everywhere, and he took a quick glance to verify that the others had woken and were running toward the exits.

Jake vaulted toward the black, double doors, slamming into them and nearly falling as they gave way to the outer room. The Caligari attendant lunged at him but fell inches short as Jake slipped past, running for all he was worth toward the lobby.

Bloodless hands reached up to grab at him from secret openings in the floor. They tore his pants and twisted the shoes from his feet, but Jake kicked himself free. As he touched the front door he caught a glimpse of the wolfish creature loping toward him at incredible speed, threads of saliva swinging from its jaws. He had just enough time to slam the door in its face. He heard it crash into it.

The darkness outside was cleaner and a welcome sight to Jake's eyes. What lurked in shadows there was the least of his worries. As he walked hurriedly away from the building he felt something crawling on his face. He swiped and captured it in his fist.

A silver moth with tiny death's-head markings on its wings fluttered between his fingers. His nails dug into his palm as he crushed it and then dropped it to the sidewalk. Wiping silvery powder on his jeans he made his way down the street, flipping open his phone to call Rita.

Evidently the desperation in his voice spoke for itself. She was off the phone and immediately on her way to meet him at a café a couple of blocks away. She told him to call the police, but he knew that was futile. He sat at a booth near the front so he could watch out the big, bay windows, eyes on the lookout for her red car and anything else that might make its way across the intersection.

His head swam with images of Kate. The despair in her eyes had been mind-numbing. He knew she would have hated that, and as he caught sight of himself in the reflection of the glass he saw three monarch butterflies flitting playfully around his head. Almost instantaneously the sadness washed away and was replaced by their contagious joy. When he turned to look at them he found nothing there but his table and the otherwise empty café. But a huge weight had been lifted from his soul. He was sure that this was a message from Kate to let him know she was fine. She had loved butterflies.

After a solid hour of him giving the details in her apartment Rita remembered to tell him she had used her spare key. A delivery had come for him. It had been an odd-shaped box, long and narrow, and she laughed as she told him she had thought he had purchased a baseball bat of his own. It had been heavy though. The delivery boy had agreed to carry it into Jake's apartment for her.

Jake's face drained white.

"Wait," Rita realized, clutching the couch with her nails, "you don't think…"

They made their way down the hall. Jake told Rita to stay behind him. The ticket stub had vanished from his coat pocket.

His keys jangled loudly from the door as Jake swung it open. The package greeted his eyes like something phenomenally out of place that begs to be dealt with. It was still wrapped. For that he was grateful.

"Got internet access on your phone?" he asked Rita.

"Yeah, why?"

He pulled the door shut, locking both deadbolts.

"I need some names and the number for the Iowa Historical Society. Then a bottle of Jack, in that order," he smiled weakly. "I need to make a belated toast. Oh, and the use of your couch for tonight. Maybe I can swap you for a box of chocolates…"

"You freak," she shook her head with a grin and pushed him toward her apartment.

Down the hall in his silent living room blood began to leak through the package.

WHAT COMES AROUND

Stopping at a convenience store well after midnight was probably the stupidest thing Gwen could do. She was aware of the danger, but a serious craving for Starbucks mocha and Cheetos made her entertain the possibility. There was a store clerk after all, and cameras, and most likely one or two other brave souls out to purchase something at that hour.

She parked under a light, locked her car up tight and hurried in, eyes sweeping the area around her. The place smelled of burned coffee and stale taquitos. An older man in a store vest with bushy eyebrows took her cash, barely even glancing up at her face. There was no one else inside, and no one at the gas pumps.

Moonlight spilled down over the parking lot in a pale sheen. As she stepped off the curb to head for her car a dark figure darted around the corner from the alley. It nearly crashed into her, and a filthy hand grabbed her shoulder.

Gwen's nostrils were assaulted by a moist, pulpy odor she couldn't identify. She lunged backward, flailing at him awkwardly with her hands with her elbows pressing her purchased items to her chest. He was a frighteningly thin man with a pockmarked face, moving in close with rabid single-mindedness. His gray eyes burned with disturbing intensity as he thrust his face forward to stare at her. Gwen grimaced as he reached into the pocket of his stained sweatshirt.

"Have you heard the word?" His raspy voice reminded her of scalded tissue.

Her mind raced with a number of dangerous and lewd possibilities, but his shaking hand fished out a battered comic book. The cover graphics were badly drawn----- characters with bulbous heads and light blue skin tones. Text was unreadable, not for the food smeared and dried on the page, but because they seemed to be letters cut and pasted from magazines, like notes sent to the police by serial killers bragging of their deeds.

He continued to dog her as she backed toward her car. She grabbed keys from her own pocket and raised them defensively, yet he seemed oblivious to everything but her face. He kept coming, eyes burning so infernally Gwen was convinced he was going to lunge.

"You can be saved," he whispered, licking his dry, thin lips. He held out the comic book, and in that moment she understood. Out of the corner of her eye she caught movement across his dirty sweatshirt. It had happened fast, but she could have sworn roaches scuttled in the layers of his grimy clothes.

"No," she managed, then half-turned and unlocked the car door faster than she had ever done in her life. He tried to climb in. Gwen quickly pushed the door into him and gained space enough as he was forced back. He made a final move and almost lost his hand as the door fastened shut. She started the engine and pealed out, watching him disappear into the shadows of the alley in her rearview mirror.

"Jesus," she shuddered, painfully aware of the risk she had taken. It could have been much worse. She had gotten off easy with that little slice of disturbed recruiting.

What religion could he have been promoting? He had to have made the comic himself, unless there was a new spin-off of Heaven's Gate out there now. She was damned lucky she wasn't tied to a cot somewhere made to drink cyanide for the arrival of the mother ship.

'Or murdered or raped,' she could hear her mother's voice say. The thought of that insect-infested thing pushing her down in the alley was somewhere Gwen's mind just didn't want to go. Realizing she was driving too fast she calmed herself and made her way carefully home. As she parked her roommate Stacy pulled into the space beside her.

"Late night for you too, huh?' Stacy asked through her driver's side window and then saw the look on Gwen's face. "What's wrong?"

Gwen waved off the concern. "No big deal, just a reality check. I ran into this really creepy guy at the convenience store on 2nd. "

"That's not the best area," Stacy nodded. Gwen was still sitting in the front seat with her door open as she gathered up the items she had bought. As Stacy joined her the girl noticed something sitting on the back seat.

"What's that?" she motioned. As Gwen caught sight of the comic pamphlet perched on the seat she stiffened. A chill shuddered through her.

"Oh God, that's what he was doing. I thought he was trying to get in."

Stacy studied her face. "Maybe he was and just had to settle for this," she suggested. She reached in and pulled out the comic, face contorting with disgust at the grime and bits of food dried on the cover.

"Hope you've had your shots," Gwen made a face.

They went inside and sat at the kitchen table. Gwen savored her frap and shared her Cheetos as Stacy grabbed a soda and went through the comic page by page. It was all about spreading the word and paving the way for a second coming. There were very few specifics. The drawings were crude and used unnatural colors and weird angles that seemed like they had sprung from a demented mind. As Gwen had first suspected, all the text was made from letters cut from magazines.

"This is disturbing," Stacy shook her head, dyed streaks of black and red hair bouncing. "I've certainly been harassed by my share of religious zealots, but nothing like this."

"What experience have you had?"

Stacy rolled her eyes. "I'm not sure you want to get me started. When I lived over on Raleigh I was without a car for a few months. I took the bus to work every morning. Most people only get the church people who come to the door. At least there you have the option not to answer it, or can say no thanks and end the conversation by shutting your door. Imagine waiting at a bus stop. You're a sitting duck. And I was amazed how often they would approach me. It was like trolling for souls. They'd drive by, see me sitting there, pull over and come at me like heat-seeking missiles."

She took a drink of her soda.

"But the worst thing was that they were like telemarketers up close and personal. I would say no politely, and they wouldn't accept that. One woman actually got in my face. It's so arrogant and disrespectful. I would get so angry. I finally threatened to call the cops and file harassment charges. That helped for a little while. I know they believe their way is the only way and unless I do too I'm damned to hell, but at this point, bring on the pitchforks. I hated the way they made me feel. Don't they realize their behavior undermines their objective? I'd be a Satanist before I joined a church that treated me with such disrespect."

"I had no idea they target people at bus stops," Gwen tidied up, throwing the drinks and wrappers in the trash. "Talk about a captive audience. There should be a law against that, especially when you say no and they keep coming."

"Exactly," Stacy stood up and stretched. "That *divine* arrogance reminds me of what happened to Native Americans. 'Hi there, your land is lovely and we want to move our families here, but by the way, you're heathens and need to be more like us'. We'll pay the karmic price for that someday. I'm just surprised it hasn't happened yet."

"Night," Gwen called sleepily as they retired to their rooms. As the hall light snapped off and bedroom doors closed softly a heavy darkness settled over the apartment.

In the stillness a faint sound of turning pages fluttered in the kitchen. A dot of blue light blinked into life on the table. Then another appeared, and yet another as the glued-on letters of the pamphlet began to glow and tremble with a faint hum. When every one was lit they surged together to form a beam of pale blue light. It oscillated for a moment, eerie and ethereal like a ghostly worm. Then it shot toward the living room, ray focusing on a window beside the front door. The latch unlocked silently and the pane slid open. The pockmarked man from the alley stepped inside, his gleaming eyes surveying the room.

He made no sound as he moved through the dark apartment. Only once did he hesitate in his mission, pausing in front of a large mirror over the couch. His thin lips formed a wry smile as he watched bustling insects emerge from skin flaps in his neck. With a soft laugh he headed for the refrigerator.

As he pulled open the door he was bathed in its weak, yellow light. He opened his mouth and a leathery appendage snaked out. In his delight he did a little excited dance as he opened the full gallon of milk and let his throbbing tongue sink to the bottom. When every seed had been deposited he left as quietly as he had come.

ALCHEMIST

SEND IN THE DRAGON

Realizing you're dead can be tricky. Standing over your own body opens a floodgate of emotions. Some souls remember the big picture and move on immediately. Some remain earthbound due to unresolved issues or stay behind briefly to screw with the living. For me there was no white light or tunnels filled with smiling relatives. No one came to lead me home.

After the rush of being incorporeal wore off I knew I needed a plan. For some reason the first thing that seemed logical was finding a psychic. I needed someone to talk to, and more specifically, someone that could hear me. In my search I left a few carefully thought out EVP's on the equipment of one paranormal investigating team in my area, hoping a quality psychic would be consulted. I was misinterpreted by the science guys; pronounced to be a murdered spirit seeking justice, and once called the D word. (That's demon for folks unfamiliar with the melodramatic sci-fi channel shows) After that I put a trip to Hollywood and the famous psychics on hold.

My next option was a cemetery. Strangely enough, those are probably some of the most peaceful places you can visit, unless there's a tour of celebrity graves. Then you can catch an eyeful, but I'm referring to the living who tour those places. What's left behind of the people buried there is more like a hint of their essence. If you stand respectfully at their stones and think of them with loving memories you may even see a flower nod to you or hear the slightest whisper of your name. But it's rare to find a lingering spirit who feels inclined to answer any questions about the great beyond.

Honestly, I began to lose hope. I had to find an alternative method to communicate. I remembered reading a theory that spirit energy could manipulate electronics. Any computer or laptop screen left open to a word program might work, but I wasn't looking to scare the crap out of anyone, tempting as it might be in some cases. So, I had to be something of a voyeur to make the most of cubicles vacated during lunch hour.

Influencing a single key was like brain surgery. It took many attempts to learn to relax and channel a smooth burst of energy to the keyboard. I experimented by leaving just a few words on the screen. At first my subjects thought they had done it themselves. After that they accused each other and the whole thing started a prank war that escalated through the company. It became obvious I wasn't going to get anywhere until I found the right person to receive my message.

A word on being dead--- I came to believe each spirit's experience is determined by the sum of their parts. What they believed in their last life; what they had done, or not done, in previous lives; one's ultimate goals--- all serve to color and flavor individual journeys. I wandered, seeking the white light, my dead relatives or even the Angel of Death himself. But I found nothing. Well, nothing other than a wry humor over the colossal joke that the Kardashians and all those other reality TV shows were renewed for additional seasons while my own life had been cancelled.

That's what one tends to see if they wander through people's living rooms at night. I stopped to pull blankets gently up around sleeping children; spoke to pets that weren't afraid of me and choreographed small signs that helped folks make realizations that added nuance to their perspective.

I believed in magic. I wanted the bells and whistles, wanted to shift between worlds and understand everything. I wanted to move on and meet whatever lay ahead. It just wasn't happening. The only conclusion I could reach was that there was something I was still meant to do.

The irony wasn't lost on me that uncertainty and indecision had played a large role during the last phase of my life. My belief system had been firmly established, but where I fit in had been a mystery. I had assumed I would get some answers once I crossed over.

Did I see other ghosts? Yes, and no. There were thousands, but not many like me. Most weren't actually spirits at all, but simple essence trapped in a time loop. Extreme emotional charges tend to imprint time and the area where they happen. Others I saw were like half-visible jellyfish that moved gracefully about. I believe they were intelligent beings, but they did not communicate with me, so left me unable to form much of a hypothesis.

Frustration made me a little crazy. I visited some of the more well-known ghost cams: The Queen Mary; Willard Library and the Paris Catacombs, trying everything I could think of to get attention. Mooning those who can't see you just doesn't deliver the same rush, but the thought of people staring at their monitors at home in hopes of a glimpse of something paranormal was too much to resist.

I was alone, as I had been in my last life. No children to watch over, and no life partner in the throes of grief to console. I had asked to be cremated. That followed true to plan without incident, and I left my small service meandering down unfamiliar streets without a friend.

It's funny what you miss. For me, having been a shy, fairly reclusive person whose human interaction of any depth came mostly over the Internet, it was my pets. For the last ten plus years I had shared my life with pet rats. They were little souls that burned brightly for a short time, smothered me with love and taught me the lesson of joy. When each one passed it was devastating, but then there was always another that came along and shared its unique, twinkling spirit. To explain that to a non rat-lover was nearly impossible, but, a soul is a soul. The deep bond I had developed with them was the treasure of my existence.

The two I had left behind had been adopted by my cousin. She was a true animal lover and I knew they would have a good home. But the others, all the others I had known and loved seemed so close now. I could feel them around me, but were somehow kept apart by a thin veil of time or space I could not breach. It was a bittersweet realization. I felt like Leothric in my favorite old Lord Dunsany tale, seeking the dragon Tharagavverug, whose spine of unearthly steel could be formed into a magical sword to cut through that which kept me from my purpose.

"Where is my dragon?" I asked of the sky, but no answer came.

If ever there was a wandering spirit blown by chance winds like a tuft of dandelion, it was I. The living were oblivious as I passed among them. Some are of course more open and sensitive than others. Now and then a perceptive face would stare in my direction or scan the room with curious eyes. I realized how some spirits could lose touch or feel alienated. I had never been much of a people person myself, and some of humankind's cruel ways were deeply disturbing. On a global level it was horrifying.

I found myself drawn to largely populated areas, strangely enough, where I could observe in my veiled anonymity. In time it became easy not to read the thoughts of people, but to sense their moods and intentions. Emotion is key, like a prism of energy quite unique to each soul. Peaceful and agitated give off different waves of color and feeling. That, combined with my new ability to move or effect small objects gave me the impetus to touch lives. I hoped that was the door through which I must pass.

Whispering in a young man's ear at a crosswalk of a hectic intersection influenced him to grab a woman's coat and pull her to safety as a car slid dangerously around the corner. Changing channels of a television rapidly in a store window caught attentions and drew people away from a power line as it fell.

In an enormous outdoor mall in Texas I was certain my time had come. The place was beautifully landscaped with lush flowers and waterfalls. Most folks in the immediate area were rushed, with trains of thought splintered in too many directions, but in decent moods. With one exception. A man in a dark sweatshirt sat very still outside the entrance of a jewelry store. There were dark circles under his eyes, and on the inside he was smoldering with rage. His heart raced like a crack hamster on a wheel. And, there was a gun hidden in his waistband.

My connection to the astral plane was not evolved enough to know how many might have died that day. All it took on my part was the small, invisible nudge of a man to make him spill his drink at the adjacent fast food restaurant. Like a domino effect, those walking by swerved to avoid the spill, moving close enough to the angry man to make him jump up, revealing the gun briefly to a plain clothes security guard. A silent call for backup and the potential hazard was peacefully removed without incident.

And yet, nothing changed. No door in the ether opened for me. I looked in vain for a white light or tunnel. I remained in my isolation, stripped of the option to savor a mocha frappuccino from Starbucks or even get a slice of pizza.

I was focusing my thoughts to move away from that place when a delicate wave of sadness wavered in the air. It reminded me of a lost ant looking for its colony. The essence originated in a young boy. He was sitting at a Dairy Queen booth with his father. There were no traces of abuse, but I knew his mother had recently passed away, and in his own grief the father had temporarily misplaced the capacity of giving his time and affection that the young son so desperately craved. I can't explain why, but my first reaction was to make one of the boy's French fries dance.

The laughter that bubbled out of him was contagious. My heart swelled. He knew something was up and looked around the food court. He didn't see me but nodded and smiled in my general direction. Distracted from his newspaper, the father raised an eyebrow to investigate. The boy laughed again as I flicked one of the tiny fry stubs left on his father's tray. It flew into a woman's hair

in the next booth and the boy convulsed with laughter. The father
hadn't seen a thing, but the heaviness in his soul melted away. It
was like watching dark clouds move away from the sun as he laughed
with his boy for the first time in months.

Tears were running down my own face. This was what my sweet
rats had taught me. To cherish the joy of each moment with those
we love, and to let it shape the way we view and touch the world. My
own heart's heaviness dissipated as I understood the gift I had been
given. My thoughts raced ahead to helping the boy treasure joy; a
sense of magic and the beauty and power of the universe, just as I
had been helped to cherish those things by unseen guides as a child.

A cool breeze rustled the flowers behind me. The sound of small,
galloping feet triggered my smile as the faces of my rats swarmed
toward me, eyes shining with remembrance and love. I basked in that
joy for a long while, calling each by name. I was thrilled to see even
the cat I had loved as a child and a wonderful old chameleon named
Spock I used to hold up to the screen door to catch flies. He had
once had the run of my apartment.

They were all with me now as they had truly always had been.
After a while they showed me my path, leading the way and
showering me with unconditional love. At the threshold stood a
colossal figure in a black mantled hood. Powerful white wings,
feathers tipped with vermilion and amethyst, swept gracefully up
into the clouds overhead. The staff of his glittering scythe was
intricately carved with a million faces. The iridescent shimmer of
peace and enlightenment was mirrored in the blade.

His face was a gruesome skull. It was a guise fashioned by the
fear of man for centuries, but the intense flame of his soul burned

pure compassion. I had been fascinated by death imagery as a child. Now I understood why. His purpose was not to frighten or cause one's end, but to help us accept and move on to the next phase of our journey. Minds limited by the belief that we were no more than a physical husk would understandably curse him.

"I see you found your dragon," he said, deep voice echoed by the warm lapping sound of a wind-tossed flame.

I smiled and nodded, rats almost falling from my shoulders, and followed him inside.

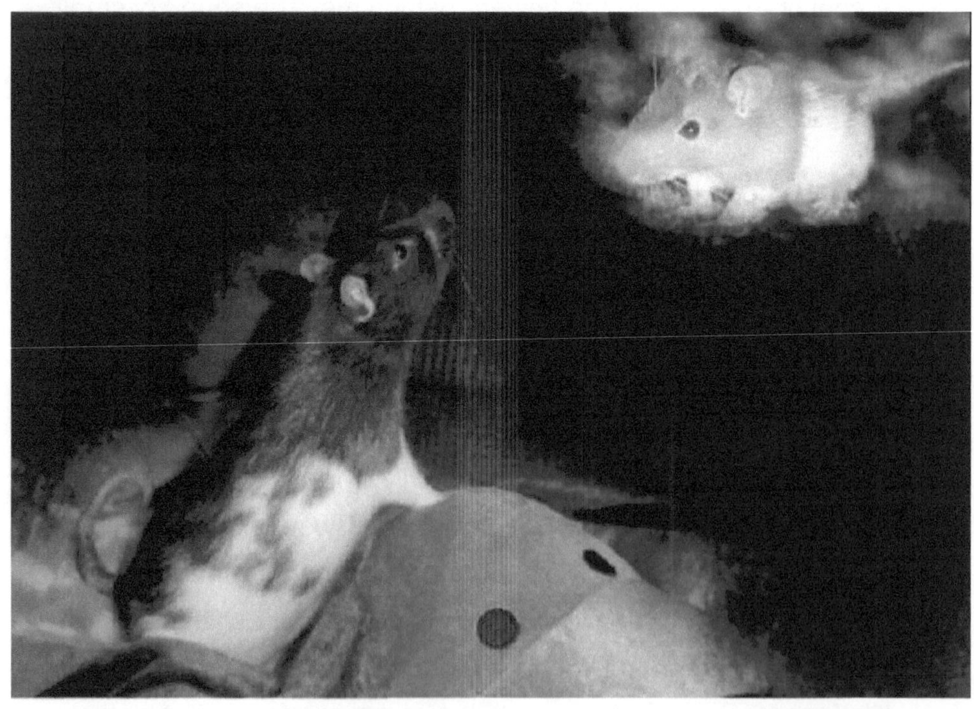

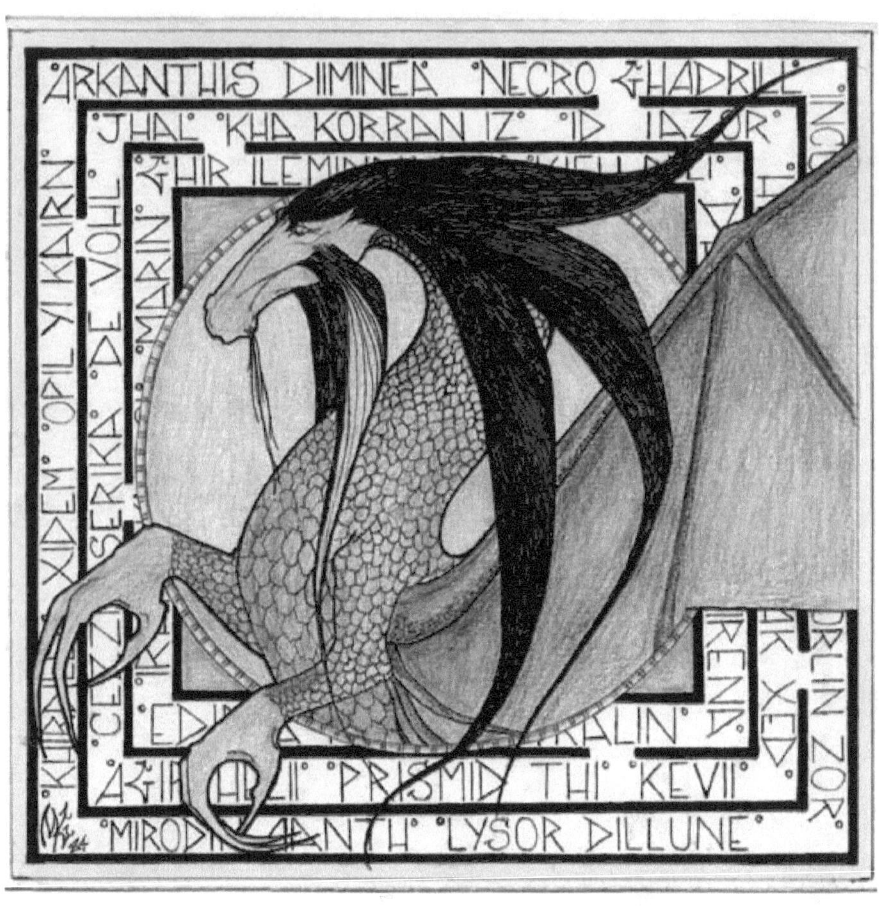

ARKANTHIS DIIMINEA NECRO GHADRILL
JHAL KHA KORRAN IZ ID IAZOR
HIR ILEMIN KIELL
MARIN
DE VOHL
SERIKA
OPIL YI KAIRN
XIDEM
CLEZ
EDIN IRALIN
ARII PRISMID THI KEVII
MIRODII ZANTH LYSOR DILLUNE

THE BOX

From the depths of a secluded lake clotted with algae something
bobbed quietly to the surface. Birds panicked in the trees and fled.
The thing floated, patiently waiting for a hiker or stray child out
wandering the wooded area behind Blue Ridge Park to spot it and
fish it from the murky water. It's hunger was building.

Dan Furness settled into a soft leather chair against the wall in
the cramped sheriff's office. The air inside was warm and stale and
smelled of coffee. Pete Reznor sat across from him at the huge
desk littered with stacks of paper, face hidden under the hood of a
chunky desk lamp. He looked up as Dan slid the zip locked baggie
toward him.

"I knew it was the area where you found that girl last month.
Figured you might want a look."

"Did you open it?"

Dan shook his head. "The kid had already touched it. His mother
flagged me down at the café down the road from there. Her husband
had the truck and she couldn't get to town. Waitress gave me the
baggie. Wasn't it a blonde you guys found?"

The sheriff ran a hand over his thin beard. "As far as we could
tell. There wasn't much left of her. This has been in the water so long

there's no chance to recover DNA," he sighed, pulling apart the sides of the baggie gingerly despite his resignation. Two long, blonde hairs were caught up in the thing and tangled around it.

"Hair's still viable though, right?"

"If roots or follicles are still attached we have a good chance. I just hope we have something to compare it to. I'll get it to Amy pronto. Thanks. You said you were in the café? Working on a new book?"

"Yeah, getting breakfast," Dan watched Pete zip the baggie up again with disappointment. "You're not gonna open that?"

The sheriff shrugged. "I let the forensic people take it from here. That lock is rusted, and if I muck something up it's my butt, you know? I appreciate you bringing it in, Dan. It'll go to the head of the line. Trust me. We kept the details of that girl's body quiet, but we're all dedicated to making sure nothing like that happens in our town again."

What if the information to make that possible is right in front of you?

The question was clamoring in his head. On his way out he passed by Amy's office but found it dark. When he inquired of her whereabouts the front desk clerk told him she would be back from vacation on Monday. It was Thursday. Among his other concerns was that the sheriff showed no interest in going back to search the area. What else might they have missed?

As he got back in his car Dan remembered he had snapped a few pictures of the thing with his camera. He kept a cheap digital in his glove box just in case something triggered a story idea while he was driving. Sometimes old abandoned houses and even oddly-twisted trees gave him scenes to throw into established story lines. The small locked thing had given him chills.

He scrolled through his photos slowly. Marie Lawrence had brought the thing her son had found into The Redneck Café. She had been clearly afraid of it. Dan had assumed that was because she knew about the murdered girl. She had wrapped the thing in an old kitchen towel, had probably done so the minute her son brought it home and mentioned its location. He had noticed she was careful not to touch it, but again had assumed she thought it important to the investigation. Maybe he had assumed too much.

First shot was when Marie had told her tale and set it on his table at the Cafe. Most of the thing was hidden under the towel. He had run out to the car to fetch his camera and not disturbed the object. For the next one he had used his fork to move the fabric away.

At first glance it might have been taken for a simple jack-in-the-box, complete with metal winding crank. That was somewhat discolored and corroded by being in the marshy water too long. But on closer examination the gaudy images on each side, even dirty and clotted with bugs and dead leaves, were nothing like clowns at all. Demons maybe, or nightmarish creatures sparked by a bad acid trip. Their ram-like horns and gleaming jaws dripped with gore. Someone had clamped a big padlock on the top section. It was rusted pretty heavily now, but Dan couldn't help wonder what that padlock was holding at bay. The box struck him as something made by the damned in a hellish sweatshop.

Marie Lawrence had said as much, then disappeared when he started snapping photos. He just turned around and she was gone, having done her duty, he supposed. Leaving him like a sucker holding a feral creature that was likely to rip his face off if given the chance. Or worse, a dark tentacle of karma waiting to steal his soul. He hadn't watched all those old Night Gallery episodes for nothing.

In responsible good faith he had turned it over to the proper authorities. It would most likely sit in a dark office over the weekend, fermenting in its own secrets. A lot could happen in that time. He could never live with himself if someone else turned up missing, or worse. Flipping a U-turn he headed back for the station. Doubt was heavy in him that he could talk Reznor into taking further action, but he had to try.

The silence was overwhelming when he pushed open the heavy glass door and let It close behind him. No ringing phones or banter or even the clack of Elizabeth's old word processor at the front desk. Weirder, there was no sign of anyone. Maybe there was a meeting going on, considering how he had just delivered a huge clue in a major case. Maybe Reznor had a plan after all.

"Hello?" he called out, walking down the hall toward interrogation. His voice echoed, bouncing off photos of decorated officers on the faded walls. Every office he peered into was uninhabited. Computer monitors displayed reports and database searches. Cups of coffee sat untouched beside desks.

"Liz?" he backtracked, heading for Reznor's office. "Pete? Anyone here?"

The green desk light still burned, throwing an emerald illumination over the room. It looked a bit messier than when he left. The metal trash can to the right of the door had been knocked over and crumpled balls of paper spilled onto the floor. Reznor's tan jacket hung halfway over the side of a chair. There was something else on the floor, maybe a coin or eraser or something that had fallen, but was hard to see in this light. Pulling out his key chain flashlight Dan dropped down to have a look, not sure why it pulled his interest. As his focused little beam spilled over it he saw it was the tip of a human finger severed cleanly just below the nail bed. It had landed straight up. A perfect thin ring of blood surrounded it.

He had seen worse, but circumstances and eerie silence made him lurch backward on his ass. Scrambling to his feet he turned to aim his light at the desk. Three large drops of blood dotted the stack of files on the left corner. Still fresh. And something sat in the center of the desk, almost completely hidden behind the clunky bankers lamp. Dan knew what was there even before his small light set it aglow. The box.

Reznor must have had a change of heart. The thing was out of the baggie and the padlock was gone. A plastic evidence bag with the blonde hair lay beside it. Bolt cutters lay across the desk chair. You could see the jagged holes in the metal where someone had punctured the top and side to clamp on the lock. Must have been one hell of a long time ago. The box made the word "old" seem laughable. If someone told him it had been there at the beginning of the world, when evil first reared its head, he would have had no qualms about accepting that theory. The prototype for jack-in-the-boxes.

Prepared to bolt Dan took a step closer. His light revealed blood along the lip of the box. Hand shaking, he watched in horror as the metal crank began to turn. That old standard, Pop Goes the Weasel, but in a haunting minor key, filled the room.

He had to act before the song finished and that lid popped open. Snatching up the box he trapped the lid against his body and held it tight with his right arm. The crank dug into his ribs but he kept it from turning as he ran from the office and back out into the main lobby. Distorted music notes rattled like metal bones scraping together. He was reaching for the front door when Liz and the sheriff suddenly loomed in the threshold. Reznor's left hand as wrapped in a fresh bandage.

"What the Hell are you doing, Furness? That's evidence!"

"What?" Dan began to stammer as Reznor's eyes glared at him. "What? I saw the blood.....everyone was gone."

"Most of them are at lunch," Liz explained as she returned to the front desk. "Pete here sliced off his fingertip trying to open that thing. I had to drive him to the hospital."

Dan's mouth hung open as he stared at them in disbelief.

"But, it was playing…" he managed at last.

"Damn writers," Reznor spat, holding out his good hand. "Give it here!"

Dan took a step back reflexively as he surrendered the box. The crank began to turn again. Eerie notes chimed as the thing rocked back and forth slightly in Reznor's open palm.

"What the hell?" formed soundlessly on the sheriff's lips. He was reaching for his baton with his bandaged hand when the final note died on the air. The lid of the box flew open.

Time seemed suspended as they stared into the open black hole. Dan finally let go of his held breath. Reznor swore. And then, simultaneously, their nostrils began to twitch as a stench of corpses and excrement and black smoke drifted up out of the depths of the box. It was a dense cloud that took on form as it lifted, towering over Reznor until the apex of it hovered against the panel ceiling. Bits of human bone and blood drops wafted from it like ash from an erupting volcano.

"Do something Pete!" Liz cried hysterically.

Reznor reached for the lid. Crimson eyes snapped open within the thing and it shot down with incredible speed. A mouth full of jagged teeth opened wide and gnashed down. Blood splattered everywhere.

In pure reflex Dan made it to his car, muscles so pumped with adrenaline he smashed into the grille. He heard Liz scream once but kept going, flying out of town without even stopping to pack his things. He threw his camera out the window into an open dumpster in Valdosta. It had been five long hours of driving. He needed gas, and food. His plan was to write a letter explaining what had happened. He would simply leave it out front at the police station. He had no hero delusions, but didn't fancy being locked away in a psychiatric ward either. As it was the sight of that feasting creature with the ring of blood around its evil smile would burn forever in his brain.

Once he had dropped off the letter he felt better. In a weak attempt to get his mind off things he focused on the old style architecture and old familiar chain stores that hadn't been updated. Some were amazing blasts from the past. Starving, he pulled into a fast-food drive-through lane. There was only a convertible mustang in front of him. The top was down to take in the warm sun. Dan could partially see the blonde in the front seat lean in to give her order, but an oversized menu blocked his view of anything more. A clicking sound and static buzzed as the intercom system opened up. Dan waited for the teenage voice to respond, but the eerie music filling the air slammed a bone-chilling fear through his chest. As his tires squealed in reverse he saw the clown head spring forward, red-rimmed mouth of razor teeth opening wide…

IN TWILIGHT THEY COME

Dusk settled over the neighborhood as brittle leaves rustled on Devon's porch. A bloody face appeared at her screen door. She peered out at the eerily glowing neighborhood of flickering jack-o-lanterns, winged demons with LED eyes, cobweb filament wafting on the cool air, and skull-shaped string lights draped from eaves. A single child stood patiently at her front door. Devon quickly scanned the yard and sidewalk, but could see no parent waiting. Her brow furrowed as she scooped up a handful of candy and gently pushed the door open.

Without making a sound the child held out a battered plastic pumpkin. It reeked of moist, black earth. Devon caught a glimpse of worms wriggling and stepped back, heart lodged in her throat. Her eyes jumped to the child's face. Blood oozed from the store-bought mask. Eyes behind the holes were dead and unblinking. Devon saw her own face reflected there. The candy dropped from her hand as porch shadows thickened and came alive in swirling, grotesque forms. She lunged for the door, unable to scream as a swarm of hungry, disembodied phantom hands clutched and hung from her like droplets of liquid wax on a candle.

Later in the evening two older boys approached the house. One wore an expensive Jason Vorhees hockey mask complete with the disfigured face underneath. The other sported gothic face paint reminiscent of Brandon Lee in *The Crow*.

"Let's check out this place," the goth gestured toward the dark house. "Sometimes people leave candy on the porch."

"In your dreams," Vorhees replied. "That's Devon Shaw's old place. She ran down a kid last Halloween, hit and run, then went home and OD'd. They can't give this house away. If you want to check it out I'll hold your candy."

As they hurried on a dark mass surged from the yard beside the faded For Sale sign and drifted slowly on the October night.

WHEN A WINDOW CLOSES, A DOOR OPENS

Rain started coming down on a dark Tuesday morning, but Kris was oblivious to it. While moving a sofa to retrieve the TV remote something had torn in her back. She felt a pop and went down like a stone. She lay there for a long while as waves of pain radiated and finally ebbed. Rising gingerly it became abundantly clear that making it in to work was not going to happen. She had done some serious damage.

Thank god she rarely took sick days. With no insurance a doctor visit was out of the question. Much as she hated to use her vacation time she asked for the rest of the week. After the weekend she *had* to be better. She did a lot of lifting. If her back didn't recover her job would be in jeopardy.

There was a flurry of activity at first. Dave swung by with muscle relaxers and drive-thru breakfast sandwiches. Lisa brought ice packs and a black emo stuffed cat. It was strangely fascinating with its white crosses for eyes and satin vest of leering skulls. A huge bag of Reese's peanut butter cups was tied to it with ribbon. Her sister came by briefly with a lecture but left Gabe's portable Playstation and a bag of games. A few friends from work called, and then silence.

Sitting upright for more than ten minutes was impossible. She managed to read her email, but then the pain was so intense she had to lay flat on the floor to keep herself from screaming. Laying there on the carpet in her shadowy bedroom she heard the rain start to come down harder. There were nuances to it that she had never noticed before. It seemed sinister as it drummed on awnings and thundered down drainpipes. She felt chilled and shuddered. That moment is when she first saw the black form glide past in the hallway.

She froze, scream lodged in her throat. From her odd, perpendicular angle she watched as the last of the black mist moved past her door and was lost from sight. Her eyes began to sting and water from the sheer uncanniness of the moment. She was pretty damned sure she had locked the deadbolt and that no one else could possibly be in the apartment.

Using the desk chair to pull herself up she leaned out into the doorway. Rain hammered the roof. It echoed eerily through the building. She had a clear view down the narrow hall and a partial of the unlit living room, but saw no one. Kris glanced about briefly for something to use as a weapon. Her eyes darted over her CD collection; a small latex rat her nephew had given her one Halloween, and her art table littered with colored pencils. Even sharpened to its finest point Burnt Umber #3 didn't scream intimidation. Her purse was right there on the desk. Grabbing her keys with the small pepper spray vial attached she headed slowly for the living room.

She couldn't remember ever being this frightened. There was too much time to think about something leaping out at her from a closet or creeping up from behind. Her hand was shaking as she held out the pepper spray. The living room seemed clear at first. She flipped on a couple of lights and slowly her brain started to register small changes around her. Most of it was subtle, just enough to make her question whether or not it had actually been moved or was the product of her own frightened imagination. The book she had been reading and left on the kitchen counter was standing upright. A paperweight her grandmother had given her years ago had been relocated from a side table to a bookcase. The lamp hanging above the coffee table was swinging slightly. She swallowed hard, hoping to ease the ache in her throat and erase the fact that someone had to have been here only moments ago.

And then she saw the Reese's bag sitting on the floor. It was still unopened, but the strange, black emo cat had disappeared.

"What the hell?"

Her eyes panned the room. Shadows seemed to ripple just ahead of her glance like eager children peeking out from their hiding places. She thought she heard giggling. It almost didn't register in her brain that she could see her breath on the air as she stepped quietly toward the kitchen.

Rain was sliding down the window pane above the sink. It formed disturbing faces in chilling detail and then dripped away, releasing her attention so that her eyes came to rest on the stuffed cat hanging by ribbon from the smoke alarm. The toy was dripping wet. A dinner plate-sized pool of water had gathered underneath it on the linoleum.

Kris grabbed at her back as it went into spasms and leaned for support against the wall. The coldness of it throbbed through her hands. She pulled away, wincing, but made herself fetch the broom and knock down the cat with her less painful left arm. The thing was completely saturated. It smelled of algae and decay. She opened her bathroom window and hurled it into the alley below, then locked the window and let herself fall in pain to the floor.

She tried dialing her sis for help but got no answer. She could feel the muscle relaxers starting to kick in. After a few minutes she didn't care much anymore and just wanted nothing more but to sleep.

Her bed was a Goldilocks nightmare. As she arranged blankets and her pillow on the floor the meds swam through her. She slowly realized the magnitude of unexplainable strangeness she had just experienced. It was as if she had been going through the motions, in the grip of paranormal jet-lag. She vaguely remembered a conversation with her aunt about such things many years ago. Now *there* was a woman who had seen her share of ghosts. Swallowing hard, Kris took comfort that her emo monster was locked out in the rain. As the meds took control of her system she drifted off to sleep.

Rain woke her. It slammed foliage against her bedroom window, accompanied by howling winds that sounded like the end of the world. Shivering, Kris pulled the blankets tighter around her. The room was immersed in thick shadows. She couldn't see her alarm clock from the floor, but she had obviously slept for hours. Not that it mattered. She wouldn't have moved now except that she needed to use the bathroom. After an excruciating struggle to get up and do her business she made her way to the window and pulled back the curtains.

Her eyes stung and began tearing. The air in the room was freezing cold. She barely noticed, gazing out her bedroom window at water. There was nothing but dark water, well above the top of her window. She might as well have been staring out the glass portal of a submarine.

Kelp drifted by like eerie phantoms in the current. Amorphous fish with numerous eyes full of sin stared back at her and vanished into the depths. The soundlessness of it all chilled her psyche, but she was transfixed, helpless as a moth bound to press up against the glass in the throes of desperation.

A distant voice in her head whispered to run for her cell phone. Her cold legs stumbled but she closed the curtain and moved away, grabbing at her back as she made it to her purse. The pain had returned, and was white-hot as a knife piercing her shoulder blade. As Kris searched for the phone a voice came from the bathroom. The faucet turned on. She thought she heard her name, but it was so quiet and subtle a whisper she couldn't be sure.

Her phone was gone. Taking the pepper spray from the pocket of her jeans she clutched it so tightly her knuckles were white. She could cheat and peer through the hinge gap of the door and saw that the room was empty. Water was still splashing from the faucet. As Kris walked in and reached to turn it off the sight of her phone at the bottom of the toilet bowl burned in her brain.

"No," she argued, closing her eyes for a moment to calm her racing heart. When she stepped back into her bedroom she spoke as if addressing the air.

"I don't know what you are, and don't care. Get out. This is my home. You are NOT welcome here and you will NOT drive me out. LEAVE NOW!"

A tapping came in answer from behind the bedroom window curtain. Her knees buckled.

She grabbed her dresser to steady herself and rapidly calculated the risk in not looking at all. It seemed like a good plan, until one by one the metal fasteners of the curtain ruptured with ringing explosion as if the material was being slowly but strongly pulled down by unseen hands.

Her apartment was still underwater. Between the window frame and the hem of hanging curtain things were swimming by that made her flesh ripple with revulsion and fear. The cruel eyes of every one burned into her with horrible suggestion. One of them opened its mouth abnormally wide to reveal the black, emo stuffed cat as it floated past.

Numb, Kris glanced down at the inside of her arms to discover letters welling with blood that had been delicately etched into her skin. "Wesley", her left arm read, as a thin blood drop fell. "Killed Me" glared angrily on her right.

Despite the pain of her back she ran. Shadow people and balls of light swarmed through her living room toward her with movements like nothing of this earth. Screaming, she pressed through them, stunned by the intensity of their coldness. She had almost made it to the front door when something pounded on it three times.

Stabbing at the air with her pepper spray she flung the door open and nearly crashed into Lisa. Her friend's eyes were huge as she recoiled from the pepper spray canister.

"Are you alright? I've been calling for the last 2 hours. What's going on?"

"Insanity," Kris breathed, relieved to not be alone. "As you can see..." she held out her arms for examination, but when she looked down found no marks at all.

She let Lisa guide her to the couch. There was no trace of anything out of the ordinary in her apartment. Everything was in its place with no sign of an intrusion. There was no water, and her dry cell phone lay on the counter.

"So what's going on?" her friend repeated. "Why didn't you answer the phone? Knocked out from the meds? And why was this out in the parking alley?"

Lisa opened her purse and pulled out the emo cat in pristine condition and held it accusingly. Kris felt a weight in her chest and leaned immediately away from the stuffed creature.

"Where did you get that?"

"If you don't like it it's cool," the girl pouted. "You don't have to chuck it out the window...."

"Where did you **buy** it?" Kris insisted, clutching her friend's arm.

"Jeez, your hands are like ice. Ok, ok, I got it at an estate sale. That old horror writer died last month and there was an ad in the paper. God, what was his name? Clifford Wesley. Was a dump of a place crammed full of memorabilia he'd had forever. The broker told me the guy had lost everything of value back in the 80's when his girlfriend was found dead. Her car went into the lake. Suspicious circumstances but nothing ever proven. Her name was Sylvia. Look, it's embroidered on the arm of this cat....."

Kris felt ice water flowing through her veins as she glanced around the apartment. There were faces everywhere. Each begged for her attention and had its own story to tell. She had Lisa pour drinks and fetch her the bag of Reese's. She was going to have some long conversations with her aunt.

THE DESPERATE ELEGANCE

Iridescent beetles scurried inside the husk of a dead tree that had fallen among the willowgrass. The crunch of them in her teeth made Gabriella shudder. But it was that, or birds, or worse yet, something larger with sad, gentle eyes that would forever send nightmares careening through every fiber of her being.

She sang a few lines to herself from Lord of the Rings, a song Samwise sang when he was alone and braving the cruel tower of Cirith Ungol in search of Frodo. It had been important to her once, in another life almost forgotten. There was a gleam in her eye as she grasp a heavy iron gate with her pale hands. Years of rust upon its intricate scrollwork and massive lock cracked open with a groan. Gabriella said a silent prayer of apology, and stepped inside. The name above the crypt door read Kirigantin.

When she had first been turned into what she now was, she remembered, she had been flooded with rage and despair. For a brief time she plotted to hunt and destroy every one of her kind, thinking they must surely flock together. But she was wrong. Vampirism required isolation. These were not honorable creatures. And they would not rise up as a dark army and fly to destroy her once word of her treachery spread. Her plan for deliverance from this eternal life had been in vain.

She cast a glance back over her shoulder at the sea of headstones. Their solemn grace never failed to move her. There had been no sign for three weeks now of the bearded young man she had frightened away. She was tolerant of many things, but vandalism and desecration was not one of them. It was a grim reminder of how she herself had been violated as she lay struggling upon her deathbed with tuberculosis. So long ago. So very long ago.

Immortal eyes adjusting to the dark crypt, Gabriella laid a palm against the coldness of the wall. There was energy even in the stones here. It calmed her. Expelling a long breath as if blowing a smoke ring she let her cares fall away and surveyed this silent domain. She had not ventured this far east in the cemetery before.

All of the other crypts she had visited had been below-ground, with stone facades opening into hill mounds green with vegetation and fungi. They were more charming, but simplistic and limited in space, and reminded her again of hobbits. This was one of a very few stand-alone structures. Stone columns on either side of the entryway were masterfully chiseled in the form of giant wolves. Their watchful eyes seemed to follow her everywhere.

Five stone steps descended to the main floor. From there Gabriella's attention was captured by a stained glass window high above on the far wall. Years of weather had darkened its motif, but tree limb had grown through the panel, scattering colored shards below. Lichen blanketed the limb as it seemed to reach downward. There were three coffins set into their resting places on the left wall.

Two were still in place on the right. One had fallen or been dragged
 down off its level. The massive lid lay askew, revealing a skeleton
with little more than fragments of cloth still clinging to it.

Carefully laid upon a small stone slab beside the coffin was a
dark red rose. Surrounding it were four white feathers as though they
were meant to represent the directions of a compass. Gabriella knelt
down to examine this. Each item was pristine, as if set in its place
only moments ago. She did not disturb anything, and scanned the
room again, still so rich with the shadows of night. But nothing more
presented itself.

During the next few hours she made herself comfortable,
gathering leaves fallen within the crypt to fashion a bed. She used
her heavy cloak as a blanket. It served quite well. Now that the storm
had moved on she could even see a few stars peeking through the
broken window overhead. She wondered how her new friend, the little
tortoiseshell cat who lived on the grounds, was doing this night.
Gabriella had pilfered a bit of tuna from one of the shops in town to
help nourish the feline with her new litter of kittens.

When sleep did not oblige her she sat beside the open coffin,
gently touching the hand of its occupant. Closing her eyes she
listened to the resonance of the bones. The soul had moved on long
ago, but there were bits and pieces of memory, and of emotional
energy of those who had visited his side after he had been lain to rest.
And most compelling of all to Gabriella, there were sparks of the death
energy. An intoxicating residue of unconditional love and purpose and
possibilities that was Death.

That was what she craved.

She wrestled with the conundrum of taking her own life. It was against everything she had come to believe. Difficulties are meant to be combated, after all, even if the odds are impossible. But she had been damned for eternity. What hope was there that her soul could ever move on?

Sighing, she returned to her makeshift bed, snuggling into the warm leaves and covering herself with the cloak. Fate had made her a monster, but she would not be made a murderer. Thus far she had kept her oath. If maintaining that became no longer possible she vowed to walk into sunlight. That was the only way. And the irony of her own words to describe vampires had not escaped her. She too, was living a desperate elegance, frantically holding onto her humanity in the midst of an insane, unacceptable existence.

When finally she drifted to sleep a spear of morning sun spilled down through the window. She would have marveled at its beauty, despite its deadly power, and seen the tortoiseshell cat creep along the lichen-furred tree limb to say goodbye. Mirrored in its green eyes was a tall, winged figure. A sound like the song of cicadas whispered as it touched her gently with its scythe.

RESIDUALS

In a dark bookstore that smelled of cigarettes and drive-by farts, Craig Valens checked out the horror aisle. Rare Lovecraft stood beside first edition Poe at insanely low prices. Glancing around him in shock and expecting some bug-eyed clerk to snarl that it was all a mistake he slid an Arkham House treasure off the shelf. A sudden wave of revulsion enveloped him.

His hands couldn't put it back on the shelf fast enough. Brain strobing with images of murder he staggered home. He knew intuitively that the previous owner had done evil, unspeakable things, and that just by being in the same house the book had absorbed that energy. He had no clue, however, that a dried, severed ear had fallen from its stained pages and landed perfectly in his coat pocket.

M. Griffith
'81

STRUMMING THE DREAMS OF THE DEAD

Silver moonlight shimmered over the thin strip of highway. Desolate land on either side was broken only with dry scrub and rock outcroppings heavy with shadow. A black Mustang sliced through the warm Arizona night. 'Fully Alive' by Flyleaf throbbed against its interior like a passenger.

Three days of driving had brought Cal this close. His grandfather's legendary cabin lay somewhere ahead in the darkness. Having a mysterious horror artist as a grandparent had sparked his own interest in fantasy and horror, but Cal had moved away and gone to college. He had exchanged a few letters with the man over the years, but nothing more. Then his parents had both been killed in a car accident two months ago. Now the cabin was his, an impersonal inheritance notification having declared him the last living relative.

Feral eyes caught the beam of his headlights and darted away. Moths splattered against his windshield and left their imprint of powdery wings. After another two miles he could make out a handmade sign. Someone had driven large, flat head nails in the shape of a skull into an 8 x 12 inch board. Underneath it more nails spelled out: Skull House Road.

Cal could barely see the gravel path winding right off the highway. He flipped on his high beams, startling something that scuttled away into scrub brush too quickly for his eyes to identify. Adrenaline quickened in his veins. He took the path and made his approach, switching CD's to take himself back in time a bit. 'Farm on the Freeway' by Jethro Tull came out of the speakers with an intoxicating intro.

The road was longer than he expected, winding deeper into a stand of pine trees that seemed to materialize out of the darkness. In forty-five minutes he had traveled from bleak desert to dense wood that seemed incredibly old and brimming with secrets. Cal knew parts of Arizona were like this, some of the historic mining towns that had become locations favored by ghost hunting groups, or adopted by artistic communities. Still, it had caught him off guard. His high beams revealed another weather-beaten skull on a wood arrow in a particularly thick patch of trees. He hoped the batteries in his flashlight were still good.

He knew he was finally getting close when a rope with realistic-looking skulls was strung overhead from huge trees on opposite sides of the road. It was an old Halloween prop. He'd seen plenty of them at frat parties. Spider webs fluttered between skulls and the rope itself was green with lichen or mold. Cal drove slowly. A gnat slammed against his cheek as he rolled down his window. The warm night air was a rich concoction of trees and earth and the spices of summer.

Shutting down the radio cut off Axl Rose in mid screech. Cal sat listening to crickets and then let the Mustang ease forward. It was the mailbox he saw first--- a classic, curbside metal box with the name Blackthorn. From there the narrow road ran on about three hundred feet to wrought iron fencing. It completely encircled the place, according to the documents he had received. Leave it to his grandfather to gird his haven with a cemetery fence.

The main gate was impressive. Intricate scrollwork formed a large, black skull that parted in the center, swinging inward to admit him once he inserted the proper key. After he drove through it sealed behind him with an echoing clang. He smiled as the opening riff to Black Sabbath's Iron Man ran through his brain.

A silhouette of cabin was barely visible against the dark sky. Cal parked under a gnarled pine, leaving his beams on and aimed toward the front porch. Grabbing his flashlight from under the front seat he searched the unfamiliar key ring again the will executor had overnighted to him. He was here at last.

"I hope I have your blessing, Grandpa," he whispered, glancing up at the pale moon half obscured by clouds.

Cal made two trips from his car to the porch, lugging his backpack, duffel bag and huge cooler carefully up the old, wooden steps. His shoulders and butt were sore from the long drive, but his mind raced with anticipation.

He wished he had spent the night in town. It was way too dark to see much of anything, and he knew there were a million intricacies here that deserved nothing less than his full attention. Power wasn't scheduled to be turned back on until tomorrow. His best move was probably to find a place to bed down and then devote the whole day to exploring.

He remembered so little. The last time his parents had allowed a visit here Cal had been 11 years old. He had always meant to come back once he got older, but teenage life and then college and work of his own had gotten in the way.

An impressive tapestry of stars shone overhead in the clean, dark sky. He drug his belongings just inside the front door, shut off his beams, grabbed a beer from his cooler and eased down onto the front porch steps. As his eyes adjusted to the night he marveled at the sounds around him. Some were close, crickets and owls and other wild things rustling in the brush. Others seem to waft in on the faint breeze from miles away. There was no discernible sound of humans at all. Not even the highway. He felt like the last man on earth.

Out of nowhere a thread of fear raced through him. He scrambled to his feet and the beer bottle fell, clattering on the steps. His eyes darted across the dark horizon of trees in front of him. There was something out there. Something close.

His breathing accelerated as he stepped inside, pulled the old screen door tight behind him and latched it, peering out through its mesh. He told himself it had to be a coyote or something indigenous to the area, but he knew better. The moment was still screaming with an odd vibe that was making his eyes water. Every cell of his being felt energized.

He spotted slight movement. Whatever it was approached slowly in a perfect line that never faltered. Skin crawled on he back of his neck. It was fairly low to the ground, perhaps no more than three or four feet tall. Bone thin. When it moved out of the shadow of the trees and starlight danced over it Cal's breath caught in his throat.

"What the hell is this?" he whispered.

It was a crudely made wooden cross. The base of it moved slowly through the earth, unfaltering as it kept coming toward the cabin. Its rippling advance left a furrow and mangled vegetation in the dark ground. It was stunningly surreal, like a nightmarish fragment of dream memory.

Cal stepped further inside and locked the heavy front door. He fumbled blindly in the cabin, running into furniture until his hands found the dusty drape of a window and pulled it aside. The cross had come to rest three feet from the porch. It stood as still and as frightening as a shark's emotionless black eyes.

His fingernails dug into the window ledge as he waited. The air was still electric but seemed colder now. He could barely make out a quilt thrown over the back of a leather armchair close by and snatched it toward him, shaking dust and potential spiders off. When he glanced back out the window the cross was gone.

Three am, the glowing dial of his watch revealed. A couple more hours until light. The resounding strangeness, hell, the impossibility of what he had just seen began to creep into his consciousness like a timid messenger afraid of consequences. He kept vigil for another forty uneventful minutes before exhaustion set in. Numb, Cal crawled over to the sagging couch, pulled the quilt over him and let sleep take him.

Daylight brought a grim disappointment. All his memories of rare edition books, collectible oddities in glass cases and fantastic horror film and literature memorabilia were blown to bits by a nasty reality check. Very little had been left undisturbed. The cabin was nearly empty. What remained, like the leather armchair with a huge slit down its center as if it had been disemboweled, and the couch with its front legs gnawed down to bare wood by something, perhaps a dog, was broken or stained and not of any market value.

He had been naïve not to expect his parents would have sold everything after his grandfather passed. Cal had been in college at the time and phone contact with them had been pleasant but minimal. Never had he pictured bare rooms with layers of dust and dead leaves and little spiders dead in corners with tiny curled up legs.

"Damn," he went from room to barren room.

He was munching on a cold pop tart when what he had seen the night before started playing at the outskirts of his brain like an oncoming headache. It was as if he had repressed it. As the oddity of it revisited slight pangs of panic fluttered in his chest. For a few moments he struggled with the possibility that he had hallucinated.

The screen door groaned as he walked out onto the porch. His beer bottle lay in a nest of pine needles on the lowest step. Nothing else seemed out of place. There were no blood drops, no Bigfoot prints, no crop circles or symbols carved into the wooden porch. He shook his head, chastising himself for his gullibility. He looked again at the spot where he had last seen the cross. It was not there. What was there, as his brows wrinkled to focus, was a fresh, deep furrow in the earth that was visible a good hundred feet past the open gate until being hidden by the shadow of trees.

He followed it to that border, glancing nervously back at the cabin. His own personal line between skepticism and belief was tenuous. He had witnessed the lengths fanatics would go in back rooms of sci-fi conventions; seen a few unexplainable oddities that still nagged at his belief system, and cherished the beauty of otherworldly books like Hodgson's *House on the Borderland.* Anything was possible, basically. Hell, Ray Bradbury had taught him that early on.

Cal lost track of distance from the cabin, but after approximately twenty minutes of walking through field and undergrowth the furrow led him to a small clearing encircled by trees. He looked, rubbed his eyes and then looked again. In the center was a grave mound marked by the wooden cross he had seen. Neighboring it were ten or twelve more, some wood and some stone, that flickered softly in and out of visibility like the Princess Leia hologram from Star Wars.

He shivered involuntarily as a chill passed through him. His eyes were watering again. The urge to run back to his car and peel out surged through his chest like an anxiety attack, but his body felt heavy and robotic. In a few brief moments his mind raced with imagined horrors, entertained the possibility of unearthing some treasure his grandfather had meant for him to find, and knew his curiosity was greater than his fear.

He walked a slow, full circle around the perimeter. His grandfather was buried at Greenwood Cemetery in Phoenix with all the rest of his family. Far from here.

Hunkering down on his haunches to look closer he realized the graves were all smaller than usual plots. Pets, perhaps? But even that wouldn't explain the slow dissolving and reappearing. He wondered if his sanity was slipping.

Cautiously, he reached out a hand toward the closest of the flickering graves. The moment his fingers passed through its cross a warm current like low voltage electricity surged through him. The grave mound rippled and an army of enormous spiders scuttled toward him.

Yelping, Cal lunged backward. They swarmed up his legs as he lay in the prickly grass. Frantic, he flailed his arms to sweep them off, and in doing so his hand passed through the ghostly stone of the grave to his right.

Rain was pelting the windshield so hard he couldn't hear the radio anymore. It began pooling in the shape of grotesque faces that were moved mechanically away by his wipers. He realized suddenly that he was not alone in the car. With eerie slowness a head started to turn toward him as an arm reached over to caress his thigh.

Dizzy and nauseous, Cal scrambled further away from the graveyard on his hands. Brambles bit into him. That may have helped his head clear, but all he knew was that he didn't want to ever see what had been sitting beside him. Reaching for him. Fighting back bile he lay vulnerable in the grass waiting for his spirit to be fully restored.

"What the fuck is this?" he muttered, staring up at the sky on his back. From that vantage the huge old trees loomed over him like giants.

When he finally felt better he glanced at his watch, but the hands had frozen at 11: 47 am. Approximately the time he had found this place, he surmised, or when his arm had passed through the first strange cross. The sun had changed position in the sky, so he must have at least lost an hour or two.

He let go a long, slow breath and returned his attention to the solid grave. It was at the head of the formation. Its cross looked older than the others, and should have been overgrown with weeds.

What caretaker could there be out here? Yet the dirt was fresh, as though whatever lay buried there had been very recently interred.

Giving the other graves a wide berth he approached carefully. Cal hadn't forgotten that it had somehow plowed its way from here to the cabin in the middle of the night. Maybe he should have been more afraid of it than the others. But it called to him. He would never be able to sound rational explaining it, but it called to him nonetheless. He had to make some sense of this.

"So what do I do?" he mumbled to himself, chewing on his bottom lip. Did he talk to it? Do something ceremonial with a handful of earth, or oh God, dig up what lay buried there? In his experience the worst case scenario was most likely the answer.

Tentatively he brushed a bit of dirt aside, ready to run if there was any movement. When nothing responded he did a full glance around the clearing. Everything seemed calm. The other markers were still flickering, but not infiltrating him. Evidently as long as he didn't interrupt their beams he was safe.

Cupping his hands he pushed into the center of the plot. The earth resisted and he stopped, overpowered suddenly with shame. Disturbing a grave was against everything he believed. Religion played no part in it, he simply thought it wrong to upset the natural balance of things.

"What the Hell am I doing?" he pulled back.

A trickle of dirt ran down the mound. Before Cal could move the grave earth shifted like sand and a tin box the size of an old Band-Aid can broke the surface. It was dented in places and heavy with rust around the lid. He was reminded of his own treasure boxes tucked secretly away under his bed as a boy. Those had housed his favorite Skeletor and Star Wars action figures and valuables like the fuzz-covered, green rubber beetle his father had once molded with his Creepy Crawler kit.

He wasn't so sure he would find his grandfather's equivalent of a Hot Wheels car out here. Silently praying not to find a body part he picked up the box and popped the lid. Looking down into its dark compartment he saw a strange amulet. Not wanting to touch it he tapped it out onto the grave.

A small bone, maybe finger or toe, Cal guessed. Dark strands of hair were wrapped around it, tied in place with kite string that looked to have been dipped in blood. There was no mistaking that it was old.

Faint buzzing sounds came from the other graves.

"Should put it back," he whispered. An incidental glance inside the can revealed something else inside. It was paper that had been folded into a small triangle.

"Not for Paper Football, I'll bet."

Soft as cloth, it felt as though it would dissolve in his hands. As he unwound its folds the small lettering grabbed his attention. The text was familiar even though he hadn't seen it for years. His own grandfather's writing, executing a binding spell of inspiration and eternal discovery.

It took a few minutes for Cal to piece the clues together. His mind raced with images of his grandfather's paintings, slowly focusing on a magazine cover he had done of spiders, and an ink sketch of a driver on a lonely highway with a lamia alongside.

These flickering icons must be his art, kept fresh and alive by magic and the rebirth of appreciation whenever someone picked up a magazine or book, or scrolled across his creations online.

Cal's mouth formed a wry smile. He scooped the amulet back into its box with the paper and wriggled it back into the earth. He felt alive with memories and inspiration. Maybe the cabin had come to him for a reason, he speculated. Maybe now he was meant to resume his own efforts at writing horror tales. Perhaps it ran in the family after all.

Halfway across the country an art dealer stumbled upon an eerie canvas. Once preliminary tests had been run to verify its authenticity he contacted buyers to announce the discovery of a previously undiscovered Blackthorn piece.

"It's quite in a different vein than that last one depicting the couple dying in a car accident with the back seat brimming with horror memorabilia and money," he explained. "This is obviously a later work. It shows a young man being dragged down into an open grave, while marking the plot is a rather ethereal, pulsing cross....."

PARTING GIFTS

Drew lifted her gaze from the Word program and stared at her open bedroom door. The presence had been so strong she fully expected to find someone standing there. Her brows furrowed as the wind howled outside, throwing dirt and debris against the window. For the first time in a year she thought about calling Shawn.

Abandoning the article for Paintstroke Magazine that was due next week and wandered out into the hall. Shadows hung like bats near the ceiling. She flashed back to the summer Shawn had taken her to Carlsbad Caverns in New Mexico. His band Dirge had been on tour with Ozzfest and had a rare couple of nights off. The Caves fascinated Shawn. One of the first songs he ever wrote, Demons of the Speleothem, was on his band's first release. If Drew hadn't put her foot down he would have gone through unscrupulous channels to have bats as pets. He had spent days searching through archaic books for the perfect names.

Letting out a long sigh she gravitated toward the sun room. Its floor and walls were bathed in an otherworldly shade of blue-tinged amber sunlight. The view was brutal, almost blinding as the sun was rising behind a stand of trees on her back property. She was amazed by the power of the windstorm as it gusted and shrieked around the house.

A large handprint on one of the windows caught her eye. The fingers were extremely long and thin. As she raised her hand up to compare size of her own hand against it the print evaporated. She blinked. It had been there, then was completely gone.

"What the…"

She glanced vaguely around the room almost expecting someone to pop out and admit playing a prank. It couldn't be. The house was pretty remote, but nothing else explained what she had just seen.

An involuntary shudder passed through her. Getting out of there quickly she pulled the door tight and stepped back out into the hall. The house was an odd mix of the furniture she had grown up with, some of her own things from the divorce settlement, and a few of Shawn's weird paintings and collectibles he simply hadn't ever retrieved. It was probably for the best that her mother had moved to Florida and left Drew the old house. Seeing Shawn's sculpture of goat skulls hanging above her antique hall tree might have sent her over the edge.

Writing off the disappearing handprint as a trick of the odd weather Drew went back to her computer. She worked for an hour and then jumped in the shower. The phone rang as she was combing out her hair. Probably couldn't get to it in time, she figured, and let the machine get it. When she came out and headed for the kitchen the message light was blinking.

Faint static hissed immediately when she pressed play. Drew turned up the volume, thinking it perhaps a bad long distance call from her mother. The spitting noises continued. She leaned over the machine, listening harder. After another few seconds she heard soft, slow breathing followed by an eerie voice.

"Help me," it whispered with despair that was chilling.

Before she could hit the stop button the message cut off. Stunned, she checked the caller ID. The number was oddly familiar, as if one she knew but hadn't seen in a long time. It nagged at her enough to make her place the call. After two rings she learned the number had been disconnected.

"How is that possible?" she mumbled.

The phone rang again, jarring her arm off the kitchen counter. It was her sister.

"In the mood to troll the antique shops?" Kyra asked with her typical cheery voice.

Relieved, Drew pictured her sister's warm smile.

"If this wind wasn't so bad it might not be a bad idea for me to get out of here for a while."

"What do you mean? What's up?"

Sharing the weirdness of her day triggered memories of other experiences she had sloughed over as her own imagination or simple idiosyncrices of the house.

"So you're saying you have a ghost?" her big sister asked.

"I have no idea what's going on. Maybe I'm just losing it," Drew admitted.

"Not," Kyra nipped that in the bud. "You're more sensitive to that sort of thing. You've always been the imaginative one..."

Drew laughed. "What else is new?"

She was the complete opposite of her sister, with dark hair and eyes compared to blonde Kyra who looked just like their Mom. Kyra was tall and athletic. Drew was an introvert. She was so short and slender that Shawn had nicknamed her Leaf because he had said a stiff breeze might send her skittering over the sidewalk. She had been teaching art at the university when they had met online in a gamer chat room. They had both been hooked on Diablo at the time, and they continued their friendship via the Internet for two years. The true common bond that had sealed the deal, however, had been their love of Konami's game for Sega: *Zombies Ate My Neighbors*.

"Phone calls from the dead is something else though."

"Stop it," Drew rolled her eyes.

"How else do you explain it? Hey, you have that expensive, new phone system connected to your kitchen PC, right? Can you play me the message?"

"Yeah. Hold on."

Even though she had already heard the voice it was still just as chilling. After playback there was heavy silence for a moment.

"Kyra?"

"I'm still here. I'll be over in about forty-five minutes, okay?"

When her sister arrived she wasn't alone. A middle-aged woman with short, red hair waited patiently in her sister's car as Kyra made a dash for the porch. The wind howled like a banshee.

"I told you that you shouldn't come out in this weather," Drew chastised, pulling her sister inside. "Who is that with you?"

Kyra lowered her face like a child hoping for parental lenience.

"Don't get mad, but I brought a psychic."

"You what?" Drew's voice raised an octave. "Kyra! All I need are the TMZ guys camped on my door. Can you imagine the jokes about a dead Goth singer's ex-wife consulting a psychic because she's seeing ghosts?"

"It's not like that. Miranda is legit and a friend. She's not in it for the money. She's here to help."

The sincerity and love in Kyra's eyes was calming.

Drew caved. "You know her well?"

"For over two years," her sister smiled. "Our girls go to dance class together."

Miranda proposed a walk-through of the house with the sisters close behind. As they were all heading up the stairs the power flickered and then died. Shadows were heavy on the stair.

"Probably the storm," Drew offered, noticing the glint of eerie storm yellow from the skylight on the psychic's silver earrings. The woman nodded and continued up the stairs. When she reached the threshold of Drew's bedroom she hesitated.

"There's something in here..."

The words were barely out of the woman's mouth when a soft breath in Drew's right ear sent her reeling. She lurched back against the wall just in time to see her sister and Miranda staring at her bedroom door. A goat-like creature complete with curling horns, sparse hair over its pale, wrinkled flesh, and eyes that glowed with a light blue electricity stood there. Filaments of bluish mist surrounded it to give it the appearance of something hung in the air from a different dimension. It was unmistakable. The oddity and shock of seeing it stung her eyes and sent currents of panic washing over her.

It disappeared suddenly, and it was as if they were all released from a spell. Drew found herself still staring at the spot where it had been, but heard her sister and the psychic comparing notes.

"That was not a nice thing," Drew whispered.

"No," Miranda agreed quietly. "No it wasn't."

Nothing else made itself known upstairs. The psychic asked to hear the answering machine tape and they made their way carefully down to the kitchen. Drew retrieved a flashlight from a drawer and her sister marveled at its bright light.

"Batteries are always dead whenever I need one."

Drew explained that she had bought fresh batteries recently because a cat had scratched at the back porch door three nights in a row. She had thought it strange since she was about a mile from the closest neighbor and had no pets of her own. She had never been able to spot it, but every morning found claw marks on the door.

"But maybe it wasn't a cat at all," the realization sunk in as she remembered standing vulnerable at the open back door calling for a lost pet in her pajamas.

Miranda listened intently to the recording. In addition to the call for help she heard a soft knocking and grunting on the tape. Afterward Drew viewed the number listed as where the call originated and checked it against the stored numbers on her cell phone. She hadn't purged anything recently and thought there might be a chance she would find it somehow. Find it she did. It was the number to a dive hotel downtown where Shawn had stayed briefly last year. He had called her once or twice from there and her phone still held the number. But it came up disconnected again.

Darkness seemed to be gathering heavily at the ceiling as the psychic asked the sisters to join her around the kitchen table. The flashlight was placed on the countertop between them, spotlight aimed at the living room door. Drew found it oddly disturbing and found herself imagining all kinds of nightmarish forms drawn by that beam.

"So the call came from one of the last places frequented by your late husband," Miranda stated softly, folding her hands in front of her on the table. "What else can you tell me?"

Anger wedged in Drew's throat at the perceived insinuation.

"It's not like that," she said defensively. "Shawn would never purposely hurt or scare me."

Kyra attempted to back her. "He had his problems, God knows. I mean, it's public record. But he loved Drew. He tried everything to get clean and come back to her. "

Drew's eyes flashed. "It's been a year. I never had any…visitation when he died. Why would I suddenly experience this weird shit now?"

Miranda smiled and shook her head slowly.

"What's changed? Something may have served as a catalyst to set it in motion. When did you first start to notice odd things happening? If we can figure out what's behind it we might diffuse it. Is this the anniversary of your husband's death perhaps?"

Drew took a slow breath to calm herself.

"No, it isn't. That passed a couple of months ago. Nothing happened then. This new stuff is fresh, maybe started about a week ago."

"There may be no connection at all. But when we lose someone dear to us, especially in a tragic way, there are often ripples of spirit communication through grief and non-acceptance."

"Huh?"

Kyra tapped her sister's hand for attention.

"Hey, I was here a week or two ago when you got a package. Wasn't it some of Shawn's things finally released by the police? What was in it?"

"I have no idea," Drew thought back. "I didn't want to dredge up all those emotions. I put it in the hall closet."

The psychic nodded. "It might be important."

Drew expelled a heavy sigh.

"He was the love of my life," she explained. "I still miss what we had when things were good. He was my best friend. It wasn't his fault. He was in a serious accident in the tour bus that caused terrible neck and back pain. He got hooked on pain killers. He tried to stop taking them. Because of that I stayed for two years. But it was hell for both of us. Toward the end he started using heavier drugs. He still wanted to break free, to get back to the life we had. But he just couldn't. When I finally left he hit bottom. They found him in that grim hotel room. There were drugs in his system, but his heart failed."

"I'm so sorry," Miranda said quietly. "It can't bring him back, but there may just be something important in that package. At the very least it may help buffer your grief."

The wind howled and shook the sliding glass door to the back patio with such force that all three of the women jumped up and moved toward the living room.

"This is getting scary," Kyra voiced the obvious. She glanced out at her car and saw the swirling dark clouds moving in front of the sun. The house was plunged into even deeper shadow.

"That can't be good."

"Stay away from the windows," Drew scolded her sister. "I'll get the package. Be right back."

"Take the flashlight," Kyra offered.

"Don't need it," Drew smiled, pulling out her Droid from a jean pocket. "Just remembered I have an LED flashlight on here."

Shawn's memory gave Drew courage as she moved quickly down the hallway. The LED was surprisingly bright, illuminating corners several feet away. She knew the goat-thing could never have come from Shawn. That scared her, and she had no idea what she would do if it appeared again. Shawn would have been fascinated, though, and she tried to find comfort in that.

The closet loomed directly ahead at the end of the hall. It was dark, rich wood. She could see a distorted image of herself there in reflective light from the Droid. The door handle turned slowly back and forth, with the metallic sound of mechanism rattling against frame. Fright made her heart skip beats at the base of her throat like a manic butterfly in her chest.

Drew's legs felt like stone. The hall had gone bitter cold and she could see her breath. Images of Shawn flashed through her brain: eating TV dinners side by side while playing Diablo II The Expansion Pack on their first date; the hint of jealousy in his eyes when she reached the secret cow bonus level before him; and their first kiss.

The doorknob stopped moving. As she started to raise her hand toward the handle the wood came alive like it was made of silly putty. Hands pushed from inside the closet, stretching the pliant door out towards her to mind-blowing extremes.

"Stop!" Drew yelled, extending her arm to shine the LED on the center of the door. The wood receded to its normal position. As she took a step nearer there was slight rippling at the top of the door that traveled slowly down its length. She watched in awe with her mouth open. When it reached halfway it pulsed outward in waves. Before she could even blink the entire door morphed into a living curtain of spiders.

Her body spasmed in revulsion as she jumped aside. Thousands of spiders the size of quarters rained down onto the dark floor and went skittering down the hall. She caught fleeting glimpses of red eyes and the claws and bristles of hydraulic legs as they streamed past her and disappeared into shadow. Her skin was still crawling she turned back to the gaping closet.

The package was where she had left it. With a deft grab to avoid the blanketed edge of her mother's Victorian mirror Drew nabbed the box and headed back toward the kitchen as a scream pierced the quiet air.

"Kyra," she whispered and nearly vaulted down the stairs, pulling herself along the railing with tensed arms. Something snaked out of the dark and tried to wrap around her waist. It was thick and clumsy. Her senses were flooded with the aromas of brine and stench that made her think of decomposing tissue as she fought it off. The cold sponginess of it made her gag.

She burst into the kitchen holding her Droid high. The light of it spilled down long enough for her to make out her sister's form sprawled on the floor. Miranda and the table flashlight were gone. Kyra's arm was bleeding and there was glass shattered all around her. The small window over the kitchen sink had been broken in, and the dry wind was howling as it punched in the swirling curtain.

As she bound Kyra's wound with a clean kitchen towel the psychic appeared from the back stairs that led to the basement. The woman's hair was wind-blown and her nice clothes splattered with what looked like greenish slime.

"Follow me," she instructed, as Drew got Kyra to her feet. "And bring the package."

Miranda led them down the uncarpeted wooden stair, brandishing a silver cross and keeping a hand on Drew's shoulder. Splats of slime and bits of rubbery green flesh speckled the floor and walls. It looked like a paint gun war, or as though something incredibly vile had exploded like a piñata.

"For whatever reason," the psychic explained as she ushered them into the basement," this unfinished cement room seems to be safe. Nothing was manifesting here. We can catch our breaths and have a look at the contents of that package."

"What's going on here?" Drew asked as they gathered on Shawn's old sofa. A spider ran down her leg and she stomped it quickly with her shoe.

"*No* idea," Miranda shook her head with wide eyes. "I've never seen anything like this. Not exactly an old fart of a ghost annoyed because of some remodeling. This is just…like a Buffy episode up close and personal."

Drew laughed. "Glad I'm not the only one who thinks so."

"Open the package already," Kyra said impatiently. She had a small cut above her left eye, looked exhausted and on the verge of shock.

Drew rummaged through a cupboard on the far side of the room and found an old can opener. When she slit open the parcel, which seemed to be a large, ornate jewelry box with blue dragons carved into its black wood, it was as if she released some unknown magic that immediately breathed tension and forbidding power into the air.

"Think we're still safe here?" Drew glanced up at the psychic.

"Work fast." She was told grimly.

Her hands trembled as she swung open the lid. The objects seemed to jump out at her frantic eyes. She gasped quietly, not fully prepared to face the last remnants of Shawn.

"Relevance?" Miranda quizzed her before she had absorbed anything.

Three objects throbbed for her attention. She touched the sterling silver Death's head watch she had bought for his birthday right after they were married. It was scratched and needed a good cleaning but was intact. Beside it lay his wallet. It was stained and the bill fold empty, but there were several photos of them together that were softened by handling. He had not forgotten her.

The last item was unfamiliar.

"What's that box?" her sister mirrored the question in her own mind.

"I've never seen it before," she picked it up gingerly. It was not something she would have expected Shawn to own. He had never had much patience for simple things. This was a cheaply made wooden box. Small. There was no design other than a crude letter C gouged into its face. It was dirty and cracked at the corners and looked like something he would have trashed. When she looked inside she found only some loose change and a couple of guitar picks.

What significance could this possibly have?

"I'm sorry," she whispered, but some faint impulse made her turn it over to examine the bottom. Something was written there, scrawled in pen. In Shawn's handwriting.

Zeke and Julie. Remember, Leaf?

He had written this to her.

Drew smiled as tears welled and rolled softly down her face. Zeke and Julie, the game characters for *Zombies Ate My Neighbors*. He had meant for her to find this. He had left her a clue.

"Well?" Kyra insisted.

Turning the box in her hands Drew saw inconsistency. There was something off about it, besides the riddle of why Shawn would keep such a thing. And then she saw. Gently pushing with her fingers she found the small knob and pried open the false bottom. A syringe fell in her lap. There was no needle attached, but its cylinder was still full of yellow liquid. Beside it was a rolled up scroll of paper held with a black rubber band.

"It's not what you think." she explained when she saw the look on her sister's face. The yellow liquid was brighter than any heroin she had ever seen, and without the telltale brown of cooking.

Drew was no expert, but she had been around more than she cared to admit. She had also done her share of research when still trying to help Shawn.

"I don't know what it is, but it must be important."

They waited as she read the note, listening to the wind howl in and out of the house through the broken window. The relative stillness of the basement was eerily disturbed as sharp talons clawed at the door.

> *If you're reading this what I tried to do failed.*
> *Last resort = big risk. Worth it to get back to you.*
> *NTK—Camorra, not the old world mafia, but a game server.*
> > *They run occult games for a game clan named*
> > *Obsidian Soul. Rumor had it they were for real and*
> > *had serious supernatural/magic powers. Approached*
> > *me with a deal—free me from chemical dependency*
> > *to use my music in their games.*
> *I said yes but had doubts. For backup I bought the plain box*
> *from an underground dealer of occult antiquities. He did the*
> *ritual and carved the C in it.*
> *Camorra gave me the dragon box to imprison my addiction.*
> *They're a serious risk and may be into demonic ritual, but I*
> *had nothing left. Have to try, Leaf….*
> *If they double-crossed me, use the C box like Pandora's in*
> *ZAMN.*
>
> > > > *Love you always,*
> > > > > *S*

"No mention of the syringe," Miranda said quietly.

"No."

"What's NTK?" Kyra asked.

"Need to know," Drew explained, wiping tears away. "And ZAMN is Zombies Ate My Neighbors. He's saying whatever Camorra did can be undone by this using this," she held up the simple wooden box.

"Bring him back?" Kyra's eyes widened.

Drew shook her head. "Based on how it works in the game I think he means to take out the evil in the immediate vicinity."

"Cleanse the house," the psychic nodded. "Trap whatever that dragon box unleashed."

"Hell with the house," Drew said darkly. "I'd rather take out Camorra."

Miranda laid a hand on Drew's shoulder as the scratching at the door grew more insistent.

"I don't think we can get out of here on our own. Do this one step at a time. The company can be dealt with once you're more prepared."

"Stay behind me," Drew cautioned as she cradled the box against her chest. The scratching stopped abruptly as she pulled open the door and stepped on the stairway. The dark hall was empty.

"Hold up my Droid, Sis," she instructed, and light from the LED bounced off the walls. Jagged claw marks ran knee level all the way up the stairs.

"Now what?"

"Kitchen," Miranda gestured. "More power there. My guess would be you sat there with the package a while thinking about Shawn before locking it away in the closet."

"You're good," Drew nodded.

"But I don't understand," Kyra muttered. "Why would they kill Shawn if they wanted his music? That wouldn't give them legal rights to it unless they made him sign something. And wasn't he worth more alive? He could have kept writing…"

"He never wrote much after he started using heavy drugs," Drew glanced back over her shoulder. "When he did it was crap. But don't worry. I'm going to check into Camorra as soon as we get out of here."

The hallway was a disturbingly quiet mess littered with leaves and papers and dirt scattered violently by the wind. They could hear a low, eerie whine of it somewhere beyond the kitchen as they approached. Drew's eyes burned from crying. Shawn's wallet, watch and the syringe were tucked safely in her pocket. Holding the C box in front of her she leaned forward to survey through the open door.

She had spent so many hours drawing at the counter as her mother made dinner. The light green walls seemed to throb with her mother's smile. They had made holiday cookies together here, and in later years sat at the table discussing Shawn. It was a treasured place, a place that now looked as if a tornado had flung everything not bolted down and smashed into almost unrecognizable bits. Kyra's blood trailed across the floor. All of it was trashed with earth and snarled vegetation from the yard. A tree limb as thick as her leg jutted through the smashed window. Deathly silence smothered the air.

Drew heard Kyra ask if it was over but held her ground, eyes scanning the room for any sign of movement. Shawn's voice whispered through her head, 'Steady, Cow Girl,' and her skin felt on fire. As she took a breath to brace herself the pantry door began opening.

She was prepared for any demon Hell could throw at her, but not the sight of her mother holding a plate of cookies with red spiders escaping from wounds on her face. Drew's heart tightened in her throat. Three days had passed since their last phone conversation. How could she be sure this was only a demonic manifestation and that her mother was still safe?

Doubt weakened her. In that moment every negative entity summoned by Camorra came out of hiding and flew toward her. In a blurred rush she saw membranous wings and jagged teeth and incorporeal beings blinking in and out of her vision. Kyra screamed and Drew whipped her head around to see a creature entirely of bone bearing down on her sister. It grabbed the Droid and smashed it and then reached for Kyra. Drew's nails clawed open the box. Biting cold crackled the air and filled it with the stench of an electrical charge as it surged forward, devouring every non-human thing in its path. As it fed on the entities it darkened like a swarm of locust. When none remained it was sucked back into the box and the lid slammed shut.

Her kitchen PC was rubble. After Miranda confirmed that the wind storm had died down Drew left the psychic to care for her sister's wound and headed back to the basement. She hid the box there for now, then made her way to her bedroom. The monitor was streaked with slime but booted successfully. She Googled Camorra, massaging the back of her tense neck as the results loaded.

The third entry was what she sought, right after the Wikipedia page for the Mafia-like secret society of Naples and a MySpace profile for a Death Metal band by the same name.

Drew clicked the link and watched the game server load. Her eyes filled with elegant text and images in deep black and reds. The site was amazing and her urge to play resurfaced. Scrolling down the list of games and enticing descriptions with screenshots made her mouth water. And then her eyes found it—currently third in popularity.

DIRGE: The Darkness Beckons

She began to feel lightheaded as she read the premise— *play as cursed band member Shawn Curry as he loses himself in a world of demons real and imagined. This first person shooter moves through breath-taking caverns filled with vampire bats, eerie gothic mansions and decrepit hotel rooms populated with junkies and nightmares. Fight to keep Curry from sinking into addiction and madness as he makes a desperate deal for his soul that unleashes a maelstrom of evil. Scored with the haunting music of Dirge.*

Anger surged through her like fire. In the upper right corner of the screen a vanishing skull graphic with the Dirge logo beneath it caught her eye. Contest of the month promised $5000 to anyone who could defeat the game and save Curry's soul. Evidently the game was so difficult (or programmed not to lose) that seasoned gamers had been unable to crack it.

Fuming, Drew opened a new window and jumped to one of the game sites she and Shawn had frequented in the old days. A quick search found little information available about the Dirge game because no one seemed to have progressed beyond the first level. The player was allotted three lives only, with no save points—areas where once achieved would become the new starting point if defeated. So three chances only to go all the way. In a difficult game that could be nearly impossible.

Mind racing, she glanced back at the screen, eyes noticing the chat links. There were no names she recognized in the Dirge chatroom, but when she scanned the list in the Diablo III room an old friend was there. Not only did he remember her, but he was somewhat familiar with the Dirge game and urged her to beware of Obsidian Soul. All he could tell her for certain was that the site and anyone connected with it was not to be trusted. They charged a large, non-refundable subscription fee for access to their games, most of which were unbeatable and nearly impossible to hack. Several rumors were circulating about darker, higher consequences and unscrupulous practices by the company.

Her friend NightGaunt was shocked, but not totally surprised to hear that OS had stolen Shawn's music. When Drew hinted that they were responsible for a more sinister, personal attack on her he offered to help with anything she might need. In that moment her plan began to take shape. He shot down the idea of hiring some of the best gamers to beat the Dirge game. What the gaming community had learned thus far was that despite it being a First Person Shooter it had proved impervious to hacks. Also, the experience was different for each individual player. Screens and sequences never repeated quite the same. The game kept changing, adapting to each attempt. As if it was alive.

Hiring lawyers to take down the company would take too long. Drew wanted a more personal, hands-on satisfaction. Shawn would have played it that way, whether it be right or wrong, and OS had already crossed way over the line. They probably couldn't be touched using traditional methods anyway.

She didn't explain to Kyra. Being attacked by ghosts and demons had done enough of a number on her sister's psyche. It had been nothing short of amazing that Kyra had consulted a psychic.

With the storm passed she took her sister home, convincing her the entire ghost thing was over. Miranda wasn't as easily fooled, but simply offered her help should Drew need her again. After that Drew spent a full but relatively peaceful three days as she carefully prepared her plan.

"Ready to rumble," NightGaunt said over the webcam. He hadn't changed much since last she saw him. Shoulder length black hair and dark, deep-set eyes so unsettling one might expect that creepy chick from The Ring to come crawling out. A new tattoo of HP Lovecraft graced his left hand, but otherwise he sported his usual tee and jeans. Today the shirt was pale blue with Rod Serling's old *Night Gallery* logo.

His provisions were laid out beside him on a wooden TV tray and in a small Styrofoam cooler. Drew smiled at the flavors of Gamers Grub, beef jerky, cold pizza, Coke and Red Bull. Age made some of those snacks out of the question for her now, and she wondered what he thought of the fruit, chicken salad and bottled water arranged around her keyboard. Memories of Shawn's choices almost made her laugh out loud. As she pictured him with his larder a moment of clarity hit her like a stunning blow between the eyes.

"Mountain Dew…" she whispered and ran to the jewelry box on her dresser. She fetched the syringe and brought it back, sitting down at her computer as Gaunt was asking if she was ok. The little color in his face drained as Drew put the syringe to her mouth and squirted a drop of its contents onto her tongue.

"I've seen a lot of strange gaming rituals over the years," he said, without changing the inflexion in his voice. "But that's a first."

A wry smile of amusement played at the corner of Drew's mouth. "It's Mountain Dew---Shawn's drink. I'll explain later."

"Ok. I'm logged in to the site and ready to go."

"Me too."

She had made sure to pay the subscription fee with a Paypal account carrying only enough for the game. Gaunt had refused to let her pay for his, saying this battle with OS was personal and for Shawn.

"Aim your cam at your monitor now," he told her. "Based on

what we already know it probably won't help, but it's worth a shot.
If my play is at all like yours I may be able to give you a head's up
here and there. This is my third attempt, so no telling what they'll
throw at me. Just try to take it slow when possible."

"Got it."

Gaunt counted down and they clicked PLAY together. Drew's
user interface loaded immediately. Her player, a damn finely drawn
and only slightly beefed version of Shawn, stood outside a dark,
forbidding entrance of a very realistic cave. He reminded Drew of
Dante in Devil May Cry, except for Shawn's flowing black mane.
The graphics promised to be spectacular.

The main section of the interface, her play area, was a primal
forest dripping with luxuriously textured vines and fronds and lichen.
Beady-eyed salamanders darted underfoot with bright red patterns
down their backs, and glowing fireflies flew past emitting low-
pitched vibrations. The cavern entrance was a cracked fissure
barely large enough to admit an adult. Primitive paintings
adorned the archway overhead in the form of eyes and odd relics.

The lower portion of the interface was typical---a section for
acquired weapons, magical talismans and potions, and the cutout
of her character enabling her to wear/hold and use desired items
one at a time. The familiarity of that design comforted her.

"Holy shit!" she heard Gaunt cry out. "Drew?"

"What's wrong?" she asked, simultaneously worried and
annoyed that a problem could hit them so fast.

"Have you stepped inside the cave yet? If you haven't, do

it. You may see some rats or bats rush toward you, but no more than that on your first play. Just step inside and look left."

She glanced at the minimized box of Gaunt's webcam image in the upper right of her monitor screen. All his snacks were still visible, but his computer chair was empty. Or seemed to be. When she looked closer she could barely make out a spectral outline of him.

"Where did you go?"

"Enter…the…cave." There was no mistaking the tension in his voice.

Drew moved her character forward. The screen went dark briefly as she stepped into the cave. When it reappeared she was looking at an incredibly realistic underground world. Shawn now carried a crude sword. As she panned left a swarm of panicking bats thundered around her with membranous wings rustling close to her face. They were like a smothering wave of darkness. She caught fleeting glances of their wild faces and wicked teeth. As the last of them whisked by, vanishing into shadowy rock formations in the distance, she saw Gaunt.

The digital version of her Goth friend was imprisoned in an ancient tree. He was fused together with its massive trunk, pale face partially visible in a large knot hole. Skeletal branches sprung from his torso, and from his legs crooked roots like witch claws about to cast some lethal spell dug into the rich black earth.

"Can't believe I forked out twenty bucks to be morphed into a dead tree," his sarcasm reminded Drew of James Marsters insolent vampire. "Now I get what happened to Nikki and Hellboy. They were trying to beat this game and went missing last week."

"How do I get you out?" she ran her Shawn character over to him with sword raised. Large beetles with iridescent wings were scuttling very close to his mouth.

"Don't chop at it!" he implored. "No telling what might happen. I've a feeling the only way you'll free me is by getting to the end. I'm afraid you're on your own, Drew. I'm sorry. But don't let this stop you. It's likely made to break your concentration. Gives me hope. They're trying too hard to discourage you. Makes me sure you're just the woman for the job."

"I can't leave you here…"

"Like hell. Get on with it. You were better than Shawn and I put together in the old days. Let yourself go. You can do it."

"Gaunt…"

"Three lives," he scolded her. "No more. One crack at it. All I can tell you is I was done in the first time by a marsh that sucked me down into hell. Was beside a stone statue of Morpheus. Watch out for that. Second time a giant pterodactyl-thing carried me to its lair and tore me into bits for her babies. She's in a cave labeled Groupies. Keep an eye peeled. Now go!"

Warm, humid mist hovered like white tendrils in the air. Drew headed east toward an ominous place on her map named Kokane. She only looked back once. It was just in time to see a bloated creature with pale, blue skin kneel down and begin rubbing itself with disturbing intent against Gaunt's tree.

She was crying without making a sound as she maneuvered through a dark tunnel. The faint strains of a Dirge song began to play. As Drew recognized it she swore. Anger resurfaced and pulsed through her veins. Demonic faces rushed at her and without thinking she hacked them savagely with Shawn's weapon. Her power and experience points jumped on the interface. She was back in the game.

Her quickness and anticipation came back to her. Evil bats spat green mucus at her as she wandered through a magnificent cavern of limestone stalactites and stalagmites. She felt dwarfed like tiny Alice in a fey wonderland that Shawn would have adored.

She reached the fifth level, acquiring talismans of power and assorted weapons and armor, before an army of albino mutants boxed her in a corner and took her first life. Re-entry deposited her in a completely different scene--- a crumbling gothic mansion. She saw no sign of Gaunt as she wandered room after room of zombies and twisted cults performing satanic rituals. A rotten parlor floor gave way and she plummeted toward frigid water where unimaginable horrors swam below the surface. Dead things floated in the water too, and Drew/Shawn narrowly avoided the fate by grasping a rope bridge as she fell past.

The further she progressed the darker, more heinous the game grew. When she finally managed to defeat a voodoo priestess and her minions in a room of mirrors dripping with blood, Drew moved Shawn through an ominous blue door.

Beyond it was insanity.

Her hand was starting to cramp as she found herself in the lobby of a heroin hotel. Emaciated figures with fevered eyes burning from dark faces peered out at her from holes in the wood walls like an infestation waiting for night to fall. Here and there spent bodies lay sprawled at impossible angles near candy and cigarette machines. A few of them were children. In a twisted homage to Psycho the front desk was manned by a cross-dressing demon who came at Drew with a knife. She felled him quickly but lost a great deal of her energy as taxidermy creatures leapt off the counter and came at her wielding rusty scalpels.

Level ten and a filthy carpet stained with blood prompted her up the stairs. All the lights along the hallway were broken. Bits of shattered glass dark with dried blood alongside police tape fallen to the floor suggested a suicide or murder. Drew was feeling her age and absence from the gaming scene when a purplish ghoul flew at her from a linen closet. Tentacles snaked out from its slit of a mouth, wrapped around her legs and dragged her down.

Shawn's character was fading fast. If she had to start over from the beginning now she knew she was done. Her hand was aching, and a third attempt would probably trap her here. She had to recover.

The thing wouldn't let her up. Drew used her sword to fend off blows. Her armor and shield were so damaged they were flashing red and about to disintegrate. She fed Shawn all the vital potions left in her dock. It barely kept him alive. In desperation her frantic eyes scanned the dark hall. A gold ring glittered on the floor to the right. She took a risk and lunged, clicking on it as the ghoul sank its teeth into Shawn's leg.

Poison surged through the character as she drug the item into play and used it, uncertain of its purpose. To Drew's relief it

was a full life recharge. She managed to drink antidote and step
back as the creature rushed at her again, three more heads
sprouting from its body. She changed weapons, noticing that
after employing the ring something else had appeared in her dock.
It was a black amulet shaped like a bat. Without questioning she
hung it around her hero's neck and swung her sword.

The creature snapped her blade in half. It smiled, tiny,
crab-like insects dripping from all of its small mouths like saliva. It
reached for her throat, talons closing around the amulet. There was
an explosion of blue smoke and a figure stood facing the ghoul. All
the muscles in Drew's face dropped in shock. Shawn stood beside
the digital characterization of himself, but dim and transparent. A
ghost.

As a loop of one of his favorite Dirge songs surged hauntingly
in the background Shawn's spirit reached into the ghoul's chest
and pulled out its heart. The thing toppled and a glimmering path
lit up on the dark carpet, leading the way down the hall. The spirit
of her husband pointed with a nod to urge her on.

Tears streamed down Drew's face. Before she could move
in the game he was gone. She sobbed, wiping her eyes to see. A
few more secondary creatures attacked her but fell easily. As she
came to the final room of the hotel she hoped this was the end.

The door swung open with a groan. Inside the grimy room
of dingy yellow curtains and stained wallpaper a motionless figure
lay sprawled on the rumpled bed. It was the dark side of her
husband, wracked with pain and addiction. Beside him were scraps
of paper scribbled with lyrics; his watch and wallet, the syringe of
Mountain Dew, and the simple box carved with the letter C.

Drew tried to go to him but an invisible barrier kept her from moving farther no more than the threshold. She watched as a shadow figure nearly as tall as the ceiling emerged from the closet. It hovered over the bed, looking down at the wasted man.

"Wake up, Zeke," Drew implored.

But this was her game. Her stored weapons were of poorer quality than her original swords and useless against the barrier. She turned her back on the room for a moment, eagerly examining the outer hall and doorway. In a small alcove she could barely make out an exit sign. There was a door underneath but not yet accessible, and most likely she would have to pass this way if Shawn was saved. She just prayed there were no damn cows…

The exit sign was peculiar, constructed of raised, wooden letters painted gold. Drew dropped her crude axe and tested the X. It wobbled against the wall and she put all her strength into it. With a deafening crack it came free and began to glow in her hand. She ran back to the room holding it aloft like a cross.

The barrier melted at its touch, folding away in undulating waves. The shadow beast snarled, letting go its hold of Shawn's left temple, and launched itself at Drew, scarlet eyes blazing from its black depths. She swung the symbol with every ounce of ferocity awakened by the atrocity of Shawn's curse, slicing the misting form down the center. Blinding light exploded from the X and the impact hurled her against the wall. Darkness fell over her eyes as thick as a theater curtain.

Head pain. Stabbing and relentless, starting at the base of her neck and reaching over across the center of her forehead. As she managed to open her eyes Drew saw Shawn sitting beside her. It was his ghost image, not the dark representation of his last year. That embodiment lay lifeless upon the bed.

"Well done, my Leaf," the spirit of her husband smiled gently. "You weakened the soul reaper enough for me to finish my work."

He held out the C box gingerly with both oscillating hands.

"Don't open it this time," he winked. "All of Camorra is trapped inside."

Shawn walked with her to the final door.

"You won't see me again, but I'll be with you," he kissed her lightly on the cheek and steered her through the door as it swung open.

In the blink of a moment Drew found herself seated at her computer staring at her unfinished Paintstroke article. The wind was whipping outside, tossing debris against her window. A slight headache was brewing at the base of her skull. She would go fetch the Ibuprofen, as soon as she took care of the curiously random but urgent need to email Shawn's old gaming buddy, James. Gaunt, they used to call him in the gaming circles.

"Where did that come from?" she asked the room. She meant the thought, but as she turned to head for the bathroom medicine chest she saw the package sitting on her dresser. She didn't remember how it got there. Maybe Kyra had brought it in yesterday during her visit. There was no return address. Inside she found a simple wooden box with a carved letter C and a short note from Shawn. She took the box to the basement and hid it well behind a loose wall board which she reaffixed with sealant. Smiling, she headed upstairs to quench a sudden craving for Mountain Dew.

CAMPFIRE TALE

"I didn't think we could top last year's Halloween camping
trip," Sam DeVane smiled as he stuffed warm graham cracker with
melted chocolate and marshmallow into his mouth. As he finished
it he swept out an arm for the group to take stock of the place.
"But thanks to an episode of Paranormal Trackers I was able to
make the arrangements in time. The asylum will be torn down
next month to make way for a new Super Wal-Mart."

Night had fallen. There was no visible moon, but the dark sky
seemed alive with a million stars. The night air was chilly and
intense. Shadows felt like primitive beasts quietly surrounding
the group of 12 ghost enthusiasts huddled around the gleaming fire.
Every now and then a chunk of wood popped, hurling sizzling
sparks upward like fiery moths.

They had pitched their tents in a large meadow fenced by
a stand of gnarled oaks. The reason for their stay lumbered like a
sleeping dinosaur against the black horizon. It was only a stone's
throw away--- a decaying ruin of psychiatric hospital where
thousands had died over the course of 50 years. Local rumors and
television notoriety had ensured its place in infamy. Curious
teenagers and amateur ghost hunters infiltrated its moldy halls on
a weekly basis. It had become increasingly dangerous on the merit
of its corrosion alone, but mysterious circumstances continued to

plague it when trespassers were found dead on two occasions.

"One of the more gruesome legends tells of a serial murderess named Helen Kirkpatrick," DeVane regaled the group. "She died in isolation and her spirit has reportedly been seen in the west wing carrying a bloody knife. She worked in a bakery downtown back in the '50's. Horrified customers started discovering human fingers and eyeballs in their baked goods. Supposedly a huge cake at a child's birthday party was cut into and revealed an entire hand. Turned out she lived in an abandoned building and was killing transients there. Cops found a horror show in her fridge."

"How much did it cost to arrange the extras, Sam?" One of the group smirked as she pointed to a window on the third floor where the weak light of a lantern had just appeared.

"What do you mean? No one's allowed in there…"

The kitchen knife sank into DeVane's left cheek as he turned to see the figure standing over him. A second move slashed upward and caught him in the Adam's apple. Bright blood spurted everywhere. Screaming group members scattered like roaches, grasping for cell phones and staggering in horror to the small diner over the hill. The waitress there listened intently with shock and sympathy as they waited for a police cruiser. She was a mousy thing in old fashioned clothes, but quick, there one minute and suddenly gone the next. She insisted everyone have coffee on the house accompanied by a slice of extra fresh apple pie.....

Fern Park, Florida, USA

1 January, 2011

All Rights Reserved

ISBN 978-0-578-07395-8